'You are driving me out of my mind!' Sarah exclaimed.

'That is what you did to me. You threw my heart back at my feet and trampled on it. Two years of torture on this earth,' Rafael intoned rawly, his sensual mouth compressed into a white line. 'No woman has ever done to me what you dared to do. When I think of how I suffered, I marvel that I stand here now and keep my hands from you . . .'

'The sole saving grace of your visit is that you now possess that capability.'

'You think I made unnatural demands of you?' he raked at her between clenched teeth. 'Every time I touched you, I was made to feel like an animal. You lay like a block of ice beneath me, tolerating my filthy desires!'

'Do you have to be so crude?'

'You are the only woman who has ever called me this...that,' he corrected in a driven undertone. 'To think that I was once enslaved by you...it makes me shudder.'

'The feeling *is* mutual.'

A FIERY BAPTISM

BY
LYNNE GRAHAM

MILLS & BOON LIMITED
ETON HOUSE   18-24 PARADISE ROAD
RICHMOND   SURREY   TW9 1SR

First published in Great Britain 1991
by Mills & Boon Limited

© Lynne Graham 1991

Australian copyright 1991
Philippine copyright 1991
This edition 1991

ISBN 0 263 77181 4

Set in Times Roman 10 on 11 pt.
01-9108-59771 C

Made and printed in Great Britain

CHAPTER ONE

'I'M REALLY not much of a party animal,' Gordon warned in the lift on the way up to Karen's apartment.

'We don't need to stay long,' Sarah said quickly. 'I just want to put in an appearance.'

He smiled down at her, his shrewd grey eyes softening. 'I wasn't complaining. Far from it,' he assured her. 'I'm looking forward to meeting Karen. If she's at all like you...'

Sarah laughed. 'She's not. Karen and I are about as different as two women could be!'

'Even so, you've been friends since you were at school together.'

He was wrong in that assumption but Sarah didn't bother to correct him. At school, Sarah and Karen had been poles apart. Popular and full of mischief, Karen had been the high-spirited centre of an admiring throng. Quiet and introverted, Sarah had been a loner, invariably on the outside of the girlish gossip sessions. Last winter she had run into Karen again quite by accident. Within ten minutes, Karen had been telling her that she had changed out of all recognition.

'I used to think you were the most awful snobbish prig, who looked down on us all,' Karen had confided bluntly some weeks after that first meeting. 'But we were really just jealous little cats. You were quite disgustingly beautiful as well as being hatefully well behaved. You matured so much faster than the rest of us. I suppose that was the problem. We were pretty cruel sometimes, weren't we?'

Listening to her, Sarah had come ridiculously close to tears. Karen recalled their schooldays with amused affection. Sarah recalled them with sharp pain. Nobody had sensed the crushing insecurity and loneliness she was concealing. Nobody had ever guessed how fiercely she had longed to be one of the crowd. From earliest childhood, Sarah had been taught to hide her feelings from others.

Her wealthy parents had adopted her as a baby. Her father was a merchant banker, her mother a lady of leisure who did nothing more strenuous than consult with her housekeeper about the seating arrangements for her dinner parties. Charles and Louise Southcott were very controlled people, physically undemonstrative and uncomfortable with any strong display of emotion. At Southcott Lodge, nobody had ever shouted or argued in Sarah's hearing. Disapproval had been signified by chilling silence. By the time she was four years old, the sound of that silence had quelled Sarah more thoroughly than the coldest rebuke. But unhappily that silence had done a lot more emotional damage.

Like any young child, Sarah had swiftly learnt how best to please her parents. She had conformed to their expectations of her. It had been unacceptable to get dirty or be untidy, even more unacceptable to fight, lose her temper or cry. In return for her obedient docility, Sarah had been rewarded with every material advantage and an inordinate amount of proud parental attention. Nothing she ever did or said had been too trivial for their notice. What age had she been before she realised that it was odd for her to have no friends in her own age-group?

Friends had never been encouraged. Her birthday parties had been well attended because an invitation to her parents' gracious country home had been prized as a sign of social acceptance in the neighbourhood. Sarah hadn't been able to unbend with other children. The ability to join in rough and tumble games or relax into the chattering, secretive intimacy of other young girls had been stolen by her antiseptic upbringing. She had attended an exclusive boarding school as a day-girl, kept scrupulously close to home, cosseted and protected by two extremely possessive parents from every potentially harmful influence.

She had grown up with an outer shell of poise that was inevitably mistaken for a maturity beyond her years. But deep down inside she had been as wound up as a spring in a dangerously tight coil. She could not have gone on indefinitely as she was...as much a free-thinking individual as a one-dimensional cardboard image. The perfect daughter, the perfect teenager, always immaculately groomed, smilingly polite and obedient. A shiver ran through her, disrupting her ruminations. She shrank from recalling the years between eighteen and twenty.

'This has to be it,' Gordon remarked, shooting her back to the present.

Karen's front door was wide open, feeding out mingled voices and music. What would Gordon make of Karen? Sarah wondered amusedly. Her friend was a successful photographer, extrovert and outspoken. Gordon was a banker, ultra-conservative in his tastes and inclined to take himself a little too seriously.

Glimpsing the casually dressed crush in the hall, Gordon frowned and curved a protective arm to her slender spine. 'We'll be standing in a smoky corner all evening,' he forecast. 'I don't think I've been to a party like this since I left adolescence behind.'

Karen gave a frantic wave and waded towards them. A long-legged brunette, she wore a spectacularly short skirt and an antique lace top that exposed plenty of smooth, tanned flesh. 'Where on earth have you been?' she demanded.

Sarah grinned. 'My babysitter got lost in her studies at the library and forgot the time. Sorry!'

'It's all right. You're forgiven. Better late than never.' Karen was running an unapologetically curious scrutiny over Gordon from the crown of his well-brushed fair head down over his tailored dinner-jacket to his knife-creased trousers. 'I suppose you already know how hard it is to prise Sarah away from her little monsters for an evening. She can't bear to miss out on a single bathtime and Beatrix Potter session,' she complained with mock severity.

'I can understand Sarah's concern. Single parents do carry double the responsibility.' As he sprang needlessly to her defence, Gordon sounded irritatingly pompous.

'Are you talking from personal experience?' Karen enquired drily.

Gordon stiffened. 'No, actually I'm not, but——'

'Gordon Frinton...Karen Chalmers,' Sarah introduced hastily as Gordon's fingers flexed with annoyance against her back. The fireworks of a personality clash were in the air.

Karen cast Gordon a glowing smile. 'Sarah has mentioned you, but when I saw you I wasn't at all sure that you *could* be Gordon,' she said, typically cryptic, as she rested a determined hand on his sleeve. 'While you go and lock your cashmere in my closet, Sarah, Gordon and I will——'

Gordon turned back to Sarah. 'Let me take your coat.'

'Don't be silly, Gordon,' Karen interposed sweetly. 'I have to show you where the drinks are stashed. You can't be in two places at once.'

Gordon was carted off whether he liked it or not. His innate good manners forbade further protest but the squared set of his shoulders spoke for him. The luminous amethyst eyes that dominated Sarah's triangular face sparkled with humour. Poor Gordon. The more aloof he was, the more outrageous Karen would be. She had already told Karen that Gordon was no more than

a casual friend but Karen wanted to check him out for
herself.

Having disposed of her coat, Sarah scanned the
spacious lowlit lounge, relieved that the room wasn't as
crowded as the hall crush had suggested. It was a very
long time since she had been at a party. Indeed if it would
not have been outright rudeness to refuse yet another of
Karen's invitations, Sarah would not have been here at
all. She was more at ease with small groups of friends
than she was amid a sea of strangers.

There was a brief lull in the music and a throaty burst
of male laughter splintered through the covering buzz
of conversation. Sarah's head jerked round on a chord
of recognition too instinctive even to be questioned. In
appalled stasis, she froze, her pupils dilated by shock.

A tall, black-haired male with boldly cast sun-bronzed
features stood in stark silhouette against the backdrop
of floor-deep uncurtained windows. As he sank fluidly
down on to the arm of a cream leather couch, he was
the confident focus of a gathering crowd.

A woman pushed past Sarah to gain entry to the room.
'Good lord, isn't that ...?'

The roaring in her eardrums drowned out the rest of
the sentence. She could not believe at first, did not want
to believe that he was real. But Rafael was breathtaking
and unforgettable. Successfully blocking him from her
every waking thought had not prevented his lithe dark
image from regularly haunting her dreams.

Absorbed faces surrounded him. Lean golden hands
sketched vivid word pictures in the air. His raw vibrance
struck her like an electrical charge. Against that intensely physical aura of his, other men simply paled into
the woodwork. Wherever Rafael went, women followed
him with their eyes. They did it openly or covertly or
even unconsciously. None of them was immune to the
storm-force potency of his personality. Or that white
lightning sexuality that could illuminate the darkest

room...burning, blatant and blinding. God had beamed benevolently on Rafael's birth but, even without that striking, hard-boned physical beauty, Rafael would have exerted a magnetic draw for her sex. He held court with the uninhibited ease of a natural extrovert.

Without warning, his chiselled profile spun in her direction. His piercing eyes narrowed, homed in on her with laserbeam velocity. Eyes tawny...hypnotic... compelling. Before she swung away on a high of mindless panic, she registered the loss of animation that stilled his dark, strong face. On wobbly legs that threatened to buckle beneath her, she pushed a driven passage back through the hall and down to the sanctuary of Karen's bedroom.

Her stomach was heaving. She fled into the adjoining bathroom and retched painfully and miserably on an empty stomach. As she gasped for breath in the stricken aftermath, it occurred to her that she had to be the only woman alive capable of reacting to Rafael with nausea and recoil.

Oh, you're so brave, so brave, Sarah. If she had known he would be here, wild horses wouldn't have dragged her out tonight. That wasn't cowardice, she reasoned weakly. You didn't forget that amount of pain, not if you lived to be a thousand, you didn't. But in five years she had changed so much; she wasn't the same person, she was a completely different woman. Are you? an inner voice gibed. He's out there ringed by fascinated, lusting females and envious, admiring males...and you are hiding in a bathroom. Dear heaven, had nothing changed after all?

A flush of shame covered her drawn cheeks. She returned to the bedroom. Backbone and pride had resurfaced, although neither was the equivalent of a burning Olympic flame. Dear lord, what was he doing here? But why shouldn't he be here? Karen had countless friends and acquaintances. There was hardly anybody who was somebody on the social scene whom Karen didn't know. However, Rafael didn't live in London, he lived abroad. Like a lush, tropical plant of the jungle variety, he thrived only in hot, sunny climates.

Her fingertips pressed to her throbbing temples. He would leave. He had seen her. Of course he would leave. Even Rafael would not have the insolent detachment to stay on. Had he been reminded that he had two children he had never seen? Never even tried to see? Trembling, she forced herself to check her appearance in the mirror. Amazingly, the sleek wings of her cornsilk hair were still smoothly looped to the back of her small head. Her strappy whisper-green dress skimmed slender curves as delicately drawn as a porcelain figurine's. Her agonised vulnerabilty was etched in her eyes alone.

A derisive echo from the past swam out of her subconscious. 'You're the pretty little doll, the fair princess they chose to elevate and create with their money. Dolls don't live and breathe, *querida*. And neither do you.'

She was torn afresh by the agony of that rejection. A doll in an elaborate costume kept sterile within plastic casing. Perfect to look at, lifeless to touch. When her life was smashed to smithereens by the man she loved, that was how Sarah had seen herself.

The door opened, startling her.

'So this is where you've got to. Here I am throwing the party of the year and you're in hiding. Thank God,' Karen pronounced in her off-beat style, shutting the door behind her. 'I've dealt with Gordon for you. I stuck him behind the bar in the kitchen, pulled off his bow-tie in case someone takes him for an official barman, and I've advised him to have a few while he's serving. He's so nicely brought up that he'll be there all night if you don't decide to rescue him!'

Sarah faced her friend, pale but composed. 'I wouldn't care to bet on that if I were you,' she quipped.

Karen peered at her. 'Are you feeling OK? You're as white as Gordon's shirtfront.'

'I had a bit of a headache. I took some tablets.' As Sarah told the lie, she went pink.

'Knowing your talent for understatement as per casual friends, you've probably got a migraine coming on. Lie down, for goodness' sake,' Karen commanded bossily, pulling up a chair and settling herself down. 'I want to hear all about Gordon.'

'Honestly, I'm fine.' Sarah sat down on the foot of the bed. 'Should you be leaving your party?'

'I've Gordon on the bar, big brother looking out for drunks and kid sister minding the music,' Karen confided. 'The food is all cold and laid out in the dining-room. As a hostess, I am superfluous.'

'You're certainly well organised.'

'Gordon,' Karen repeated impatiently. 'You've been holding out on me. Who? Where? How? I would have had to pin him to the wall and throw knives to get the details out of him! Even then, it might just have been name, rank and number. Still, he looks exactly what protective Mummy and Daddy Southcott would prescribe for an unattached daughter.'

Rafael would be gone when she returned to the party. Bolstered by the conviction, Sarah's rigid spine relaxed slightly. 'He's a banker.'

'I knew it!' Karen carolled with exuberant satisfaction. 'I said to him, you're a broker, an accountant or a tax consultant. He didn't look at all pleased, but he's got a face like a bank vault! Without the magic combination, you stay out in the cold.'

Karen's madcap conversation was steadily easing Sarah's tension. 'We *are* just friends. He recently transferred here from New York. He's a widower. His wife died of leukaemia last year,' she related ruefully. 'Understandably he's not over that yet. It must have been harrowing for him.'

Karen was aghast. 'Oh, no!' she groaned. 'I'll have to take him off the bar now! No wonder he looked so grim when I was reduced to my tinker, tailor rhyme and came up with undertaker.' Her friend's embarrassment ebbed fast and her generous mouth slowly upcurved again. 'But on the other hand, I'd say that Gordon is coping with his tragic loss rather better than you suspect. The one time he didn't look as locked up as a bank vault was when I was trailing him away from you. Gordon, my pet, is half in love with you already!'

Sarah stared at her in astonishment. 'Of course he isn't. I hardly know him. He's spent a couple of weekends with my parents. We've lunched once or twice, gone to the theatre...that's all.'

Karen shook her head in exasperation. 'You're dating him, Sarah. You just haven't noticed yet.'

'You don't understand,' Sarah protested uneasily.

'Casual acquaintances aren't as protective as guard dogs,' Karen teased. 'And you are far too beautiful to inspire purely platonic thoughts. Why should that be a problem?'

'Gordon and I have been quite frank with each other, Karen.' Sarah was maintaining her amused smile with difficulty. 'Neither of us is interested in emotional involvement. I like him but that really is all there is to it.'

'He's handsome, successful and free and the best you can do is like the guy?' Karen was quite appalled by the admission. 'What am I going to do with you? Is this the female who knocked our entire school on its ear by eloping with an exceptionally ineligible foreigner in Upper Sixth? You went out in style, my pet. What happened to all that risk-taking passion and spontaneity?'

Sarah's facial muscles locked, what colour she had recovered evaporating. 'I grew up,' she muttered tightly.

'No. You buried yourself,' Karen argued. 'Look, I've never pressed you...well, not seriously pressed, for a single gory detail about your marriage. I know it must have been very painful because if it hadn't been you'd have been able to talk about it by now. But there's more to life than motherhood, Sarah. Goodness knows, everyone's allowed to make one mistake. First time round you obviously landed a prize bastard. So what? I don't think I'd have done much better choosing a life partner at eighteen, but you don't let one bad experience put you into permanent retirement!'

'Lecture over?' Sarah prompted. A drink or two and Karen became a crusader. Unfortunately Karen just didn't know what she was talking about.

Venting a rather rude word, Karen leapt up to renew her lipstick at the mirror. 'You don't know how lucky you are. Gordon's cute. I fancied him the instant I laid eyes on him!'

Sarah's taut mouth twitched. 'Feel free.'

Karen sent her a wry glance. 'I'd need a rope and tackle. He's taken. And he's tailor-made for you. At least give him a chance.'

The idea that Gordon might actually want that chance disturbed Sarah. Could Karen be right? Her friend was surprisingly perceptive about people. Her snap judgements were often spot on. If Karen was right about Gordon, Sarah would have to stop seeing him.

'Holy Moses! I've a head like a sieve!' Karen gasped, comic dismay widening her eyes. 'I forgot about my celebrity guest. What are we doing in here? One of the models I worked with in Italy simply walked in with him as cool as you please. Rafael Alejandro! Here! In my humble home. Can you believe that?'

Deception didn't come naturally to Sarah. 'Alejandro...the painter?'

'Dear God, is there another one around? He's only one of the most famous artists alive!' Karen stressed. 'Considering that most of them have to drop dead to achieve recognition, we are talking here about fame as in serious fame, fame with a capital F!'

'I believe he's a remarkably talented artist.' Even to her own ears, Sarah sounded wooden.

'Believe me, when you look at him his skill with a paintbrush is about the last thing on your mind.' Karen was dry, annoyed by Sarah's refusal to be impressed. 'Newsprint doesn't do him justice.'

'The gossip columns do.'

Karen dropped her offended stare and grinned. 'Sarah, my innocent, when you get an incredibly beautiful man the wild reputation goes with the territory. "Mad, bad and dangerous to know" may not be you but you haven't seen him yet. The guy is pure fantasy. I swear my hormones went into a feeding frenzy on the doorstep!'

As Sarah stood up, her conscience twanged. Sarah would be upset when she found that the rare bird had flown in her absence. 'More you than Gordon?'

'No. I like to appreciate but I've no ambition to touch... well, at least not in my sane mind,' Karen confided with her usual devotion to the absolute truth. 'I prefer my men less... what do they call it in Spain? *Muy hombre?* A volatile artistic genius would be much too unpredictable for me.'

In actuality, Rafael was not unpredictable, Sarah reflected helplessly. He did what he wanted, when he wanted, how he wanted. He had a tongue like a whip and a convoluted, brilliant mind that thought round corners into the dark, secret places other people sensibly left alone.

'Anyway, he's reputed to be fantastically clever as well,' Karen rattled on. 'I'm not running myself down but I'm no Einstein and you just couldn't be in control with a guy like that. It's fatuous but people will talk about this party forever simply because he's here.' Karen pulled open the door to find Gordon raising a hand to knock on it. Half amused, half irritated, she said, 'I underestimated you. Have you got a homing device planted on her?'

Gordon smiled and looked through her simultaneously. Karen flushed and muttered something about food in the oven.

'Sorry, was I ages? We got caught up,' Sarah said lightly.

'I got taken over,' Gordon shared wryly. 'You were right. She's not at all like you. She's like a great over-grown schoolgirl.'

'She's a lovely person and there's not an ounce of malice in her.'

Reluctantly he smiled. 'Can you imagine the havoc she'd wreak if there were? Her brain is two steps behind her conversation.'

'I wonder why she thought you were cute.'

'Cute?' His nostrils flared fastidiously.

'A compliment you do not deserve.'

Unexpectedly he laughed, his pugnacious aspect vanishing. 'I think of fluffy toys as cute but I was out of order. Let's grab a seat,' he suggested.

Gordon being Gordon there was no need to grab or even to search. He guided her between a low table and sofa, stowing her down in one corner. Ten seconds later he reappeared with two drinks he had evidently stashed somewhere near by in readiness. Gordon was always well organised. Meeting the level scrutiny she had been self-consciously evading, Sarah smiled. For once, Karen had made a mistake. Purely platonic friendship was perfectly possible between sensible people.

Her wandering gaze suddenly jolted to a halt. Shock reverberated through her in sickening waves and her fingers curled into her evening bag like white-knuckled talons, bracing for attack.

Rafael was lounging on the matching sofa on the other side of the low table. Her throat closed over. Every long lean line of his magnificent body emanated unnatural relaxation. There was a reckless violence in the dark, glittering stare that entrapped hers across the divide. Her ability to breathe was suffocated at source.

'The punch has the kick of a mule,' Gordon told her warningly.

Half of it went down Sarah's convulsed throat in one go. Rafael had switched his attention back to the sinuous redhead curled under his arm. Cerise-painted fingertips were idly tracing the taut inner seam of the faded denim encasing one long, muscular thigh. Those caressing fingers exercised a sick fascination over Sarah. She could not take her eyes off them.

Gordon was talking to her and she couldn't hear him. In desperation she turned towards him, only to be nailed again by Rafael's steel-bright stare. Unforgivably he had been watching her watching him. She felt like an animal caught cruelly in the jaws of a trap with the hunter standing over her, making no attempt to administer a clean kill. She had the terrifying sensation that Rafael was seeing her naked and defenceless. Her muscles were so clenched that she physically hurt. For a crazed moment she was so wildly out of control that she almost ran for cover again.

Karen's voice exploded in her ear. 'Why aren't you circulating?'

Karen wasn't real. Gordon wasn't real. The only reality was Rafael, even when Karen was blocking her view. He had not needed to speak to brutally intimate his savage contempt for her as a woman. He only had to sit there letting that tramp practically make love to him in public! She read the message like the banner he intended it to be and she felt ill, cornered.

'*Por dios,* this world is truly a small place.' Sarah's head jerked up, a row of spectral toothmarks biting into her jangled nerves, her pallor pronounced.

Rafael had moved. He stood over her now, casting a long dark shadow before he crouched down in front of her with a natural athlete's grace. So close, so unexpected was it that it took every atom of will-power she possessed not to rear back. Somewhere Karen was loudly proclaiming an introduction.

'Sarah and I know each other.' He said it to her, nobody else, his tiger's eyes a golden threat on her white immobility.

'You know each other?' Karen positively squealed, hanging over the back of the sofa. 'Where from?'

A smile slashed Rafael's expressive mouth. A long brown forefinger skated over Sarah's fiercely clenched hands, a mountain cat taking a first playful swipe at a trapped prey, frozen with fear. 'Where from?' he prompted silky soft. 'Am I so easily, so quickly forgotten?'

Only desperation came to her rescue. 'Paris, wasn't it?' she managed tautly.

'When I was still starving in my garret, although not alone,' he mocked, velvety smooth, smiling again as her trembling fingers snaked jerkily back out of reach. 'I believe I was part of the Francophile experience.' Slowly he sprang upright again, still ignoring Gordon. *'Es verdad?'*

'Boy, have you got some explaining to do!' Karen snapped painfully close to her eardrum as he walked away. 'Give me an inch, Gordon, there's a love. This is girl-talk, utterly beneath your notice. Sarah, you couldn't possibly have forgotten him!'

'To think that I once believed that the Spanish were a uniquely courteous race,' Gordon drawled. 'Shall we sample supper?'

Karen cut in on him, 'Sarah, tell me——'

'You don't need a public address system, do you?' Gordon detached Sarah's numbed arm from Karen's over-enthusiastic grip. They were a hair's breadth from fighting over her, Sarah realised on the brink of hysteria. Rafael's behaviour had shocked her into dumb stupidity. She couldn't have made small talk to save her life.

'Paris,' said Karen and suddenly she burst out laughing. 'Of course! He was one of Margo's and you never did tell tales.'

Karen had herded them both into the dining-room. She was chatting nineteen to the dozen now, glad to have solved the mystery so easily. 'We all thought it was a scream when Sarah's parents let her go and stay in Paris with Margo. Easter in Upper Sixth, wasn't it?'

Gordon passed out plates. 'Margo?' he prompted obediently.

Sarah parted bone-dry lips. 'Margo Carruthers. Her father had an engineering business in Paris.'

'Sarah used to sleep in French class,' Karen took up impatiently. 'And her parents put French on a level with flower arranging and good carriage.'

'I went to Paris to improve my French.' Sarah had to fight to keep her voice level on the unnecessary explanation.

Karen was giggling like a drain.

'I'm afraid I don't see the joke,' Gordon imparted.

Karen gave him a 'you-wouldn't' look. 'Margo was sex mad. Anything in trousers,' she emphasised. 'But she acted like a little novice nun round parents. You must know what the Southcotts are like. If they'd had a clue what Margo's favourite pursuit was, they'd never have let Sarah within a mile of her exclusive company!'

'Teenagers are very vulnerable,' Gordon said coolly.

'You can't know the Southcotts very well. When there was a flu outbreak at school, they kept Sarah home for a whole six weeks!' Karen sent Sarah's shuttered face a guilty glance. 'Sorry, forgot you were there. Where are you in this conversation, anyway?'

Karen's sister came up and whispered something. 'No!' Karen exclaimed in angry vexation. 'Excuse me. Someone's been in my dark-room.'

'I hope we can assume that the interrogation is over,' Gordon said grimly. 'Alejandro had one hell of a nerve forcing himself on you like that. But then what can you expect from a gypsy?'

An extraordinary urge to slap the complacent superiority from Gordon's well-bred features assailed Sarah. Karen's assumption that Rafael had been one of Margo's men had filled her with embittered humour. Even her closest friend couldn't imagine any more intimate connection between them. Only the devil's idea of a black joke could have matched two such radically different personalities. And why had she had to go to hell and back to discover what was so obvious to everyone else? The North Pole and the equator did not meet.

Gordon hailed a familiar face with relief. Another dinner-jacket and bow-tie. A man with a thin blonde on his arm shook her hand, spoke, and she must have spoken back. The dialogue roamed from government cuts to the Booker Prize on to Wall Street. Gordon was in his element. They worked their passage slowly back to the lounge, a comfortable part of a foursome, but shock was still curdling Sarah's stomach. Nervous tension always made her feel sick.

Rafael was leaning back against the wall. He didn't have a restful bone in his superbly built body. He was never still even when he was working. Oh, God...oh... In despair, she struggled to suppress the memories chipping away at what little remained of her poise. As people pushed past, propelling her uncomfortably closer to Rafael, Gordon draped an unexpected arm round her narrow shoulders. Rafael's lady friend was tugging at his sleeve, her other hand resting on his chest. Sarah was reminded of a red setter bouncing up and down with a lead in its mouth, begging for a walk. Repulsion slithered through her. Some cruel fate had decided to punish her tonight.

'I think it's time we went home.' It was Gordon's clipped drawl.

'Yes, it's getting late.' She had no idea what time it was, how long it might have been since she had finally contrived to wrench her magnetised attention from Rafael.

Gordon steered her out to the hall with surprising speed. 'I'll collect your coat.'

A chill was spreading along her veins. She would phone Karen tomorrow. In all likelihood, Karen would not even recall that she had left without speaking to her. Before she could take refuge in that hope, Karen emerged from the lounge and hurried over to her.

'Will someone please tell me what was going on in there?' she hissed.

'Sorry, I don't ...'

'Gordon and Rafael Alejandro. For a minute I thought there might be a punch-up but Gordon predictably opted for the diplomatic retreat. Talk about instant antipathy and not a word exchanged!' Karen giggled. 'You don't mean to say you didn't notice all that silent flexing of male egos? You're blind, Sarah.'

Gordon appeared in the midst of these unwelcome confidences. Smoothly cutting in on Karen, he mentioned an early morning meeting with just the right touch of polished regret.

'Phone me when you get home,' Karen mouthed, unimpressed.

There was silence in the lift. Her high heels clicked noisily over the pavement. Gordon unlocked the passenger door of his Porsche. Her hands were trembling. She clasped them together on her lap. When a taxi cut in front of them, Gordon cursed, which was most unlike him.

'It was you in Paris with Alejandro,' he murmured flatly, abruptly.

Sarah shut her eyes. 'Yes.'

Silence stretched but mentally she imagined that she heard the crash as she fell off her ladylike pedestal.

'Just yes?' Gordon queried, crunching the gears at the traffic lights. He was revealing a flip side character unfamiliar to her. 'It's none of my business, but he upset you.'

She straightened out her coiled fingers, rearranging her hands with the care of a small child mindful of adult appraisal. 'I'm not very good with surprise encounters. I didn't expect to ever see him again.'

'You were still at school! What kind of a...?' His voice broke off harshly.

Sooner or later, Gordon and Karen would both add two and two and make four. She had fallen in love when she was eighteen. Love had sent her off the rails. Love had plunged her into a kind of compulsive insanity that had left her at the mercy of emotions she could neither understand nor control.

For the first time in her life, someone had had more power over her than her parents. The Southcotts had been faced with someone as strong-willed, as ruthlessly manipulative and possessive as they were themselves. Battle had commenced with a vengeance. Stranded in the middle of the war zone, already sinking beneath the pressures of a relationship in which she was hopelessly out of her depth, Sarah had slowly been torn in two.

Rafael was the estranged and unrepentantly unfaithful husband who had had the unmitigated gall to refuse her a divorce. The high-powered lawyer her father had hired had tried repeatedly to break the deadlock. He had failed. Had Sarah been prepared to prove Rafael's adultery, she would not have required his consent to a divorce. But Sarah had not been prepared to grasp that stinging nettle. Indeed she had shrunk from the threat of the publicity that would have accompanied a contested case. And three months from now the five-year time limit would be up. Technical freedom would be hers once more.

And what difference would it make to her? Sarah had stopped feeling married in the white-walled prison of a luxurious private clinic while she had waited . . . and she waited for a man who never arrived. What did it do to a woman when she offered understanding, if not forgiveness, and even understanding was rejected? Why had she even bothered to write to him? Time and time again she had asked herself that question. In her darkest hour she had offered an olive branch . . . in her own parlance, she had crawled. Her husband had committed adultery. And she had crawled. For nothing. That was what was still burned into her soul. She had put her pride on the line for nothing.

It was a blessing that nobody knew his identity. Her parents had gone to great lengths right from the beginning to bury all the evidence. When she had failed to return from Paris, they had told the school that she was ill and when time wore on that she was convalescing abroad. Rafael's starburst ascent from impoverishment to success beyond anyone's wildest dreams was a savage irony. 'An offence against good taste,' her mother had called it.

She rested her aching head back while Gordon drove her home to her small Kensington flat. 'I wish you'd talk to me,' he said.

'I'm sorry.'

At the door of her flat, he caught her wrist between his fingers. Suddenly he was kissing her, the pressure of his mouth warm and practised on hers. She endured the embrace passively. Unmoving, unresponsive. To respond you had to feel something. Sarah felt nothing beyond an awkward sense of embarrassment.

Gordon drew back, a faint flush on his cheekbones. 'I don't win any prizes for timing, do I?' But he smiled down at her, restored to his normally even temper. 'I'll call you.'

Karen had once told her that no man ever believed his interest might be unwelcome to a woman. And Gordon was a very confident man, calmly proving the concept. At the start of the evening the mere idea of Gordon kissing her would have been enough to alarm Sarah, but Rafael had already sent her crashing through the shock barrier.

'I'll be very busy this week,' she replied.

His mouth quirked but he said nothing, standing there until she was safely indoors. Dropping her coat on the hall chair, she kicked off her shoes and walked into the lounge.

Her babysitter was already bundling up her books. 'You're early. I didn't expect you for ages yet.'

'I was tired.' Sarah dug into her purse and paid the teenager, who lived just across the corridor. 'Any problems?'

'Oh, no!' Angela grinned, digging the notes deep into the pocket of her skin-tight jeans. 'I let them watch the late film with me,' she then conceded carelessly. 'I'll let myself out.'

Sarah wandered over to the sideboard and withdrew the bottle of brandy which she kept for her father's occasional consumption. She was pouring a measure into a crystal glass when she thought she heard Angela speaking to someone. With a frown she lifted her head just as the front door rocked on the teenager's noisy slam, making her wince.

Angela was trustworthy and sensible but she had a soft-hearted tendency to give way to Gilly and Ben's pleas to get back out of bed. Give the twins an inch and they took a mile. Tomorrow they would be overtired and cross. Tomorrow . . . her hand shook and she curved an arm over her stomach. Damn him, damn him . . . damn him.

'*Dios mio.*' It was a purred intervention in the quiet. 'I should think you would need to drain the bottle to sleep tonight.'

Incredulously, she whirled round. The glass slid between her fingers and fell with a soft thud, spilling out an amber pool of liquid in a slowly spreading stain on the carpet.

CHAPTER TWO

'LO SIENTO. I'm sorry. Did I startle you?' Grimly amused
by the entrance he had achieved, Rafael uncoiled his lean
length from the doorway. He executed the motion with
inherent animal grace, strolling soundlessly into the
lamplight out of the shadows. From beneath luxuriant
black lashes that a woman would have killed to possess,
narrowed tiger's eyes inspected her. 'It is so unlike you
to be clumsy.'

Her tongue unglued from the roof of her mouth. 'How
did you get in?'

'The girl was leaving. I told her I was awaited. She
was surprised but very trusting.' Even white teeth flashed
against golden skin. 'You have this one trait which I can
appreciate now. There was no risk that I would be
breaking up a private party for two. You really should
tell that pretty tailor's dummy that he's on to a very bad
bet; I might almost find it within my heart to pity him.'

She could barely follow what he was saying to her.
Over four years of silence and then this? Why should
Rafael come here now? It made no sense. Her violet
eyes were huge against her pallor. 'How did you find
out where I lived?'

'That wasn't difficult.' His hard mouth twisted.

'What do you want?' she demanded shakily.

A broad shoulder sheathed in butter-soft leather
shifted in an infinitesimal shrug. 'I don't know. Perhaps
I was curious.'

'Curious?' she echoed, her voice rising steeply.

He glanced round the small, pleasantly furnished
room. 'This is not how I pictured you living,' he ad-

26

mitted. 'I would picture you in the drawing-room at your parents' home, a butterfly safely preserved behind glass.'

Dialogue with Rafael had never been straightforward. He had a disorientating habit of leaping back and forth, voicing exactly what passed through his agile mind. Jerkily she folded her arms. He bent a long-fingered hand down to the corner of the armchair beside him, twitching up something that had caught his attention. It was a cookery book. 'You use this?' he asked, much as if it were a mechanic's wrench.

Perspiration was dampening her skin. Hysteria was clawing at her. She was too afraid to make sense of his sudden impulsive appearance. 'Any reason why I shouldn't?' she enquired defensively.

Casting the item carelessly aside again, he straightened to his full six feet two inches. 'When you stand like that, you look like a little fishwife. Mama wouldn't like it,' he said cruelly. 'Who takes care of you here?'

The blood rushed hotly to her cheeks. 'Nobody.'

'You have learnt to cook and clean? You astonish me.'

'If you don't get out of here, I'll call the police!' she threatened in a wild rush.

Rafael dealt her an unmoved glance of contempt. 'I am still your husband. If I want to be here, I have the right to be here.'

'No! You do not have that right!'

'You should be calm. One may have the right without the desire to exercise it for very long,' he sliced back. 'Why do you live in a place like this? Don't tell me— Papa's finally been caught insider dealing!'

Agonising tension was squaring her slight shoulders. 'I meant what I said. If you don't leave, I'll——'

Rafael bit out a sardonic laugh. 'Why not? Call the police and entertain me. It is the emptiest threat of all and you know it. You would not court the publicity.'

'Wouldn't I?' He had moved slightly closer and she took a tiny uncertain step backwards, her pale head gradually lowering in defeat. 'No, I wouldn't.'

'I don't understand why you should be so afraid.' He paused, brilliant golden eyes clashing with her upward glance in naked enmity. 'What a lie! You have the intelligence to be afraid. But what of? Violence may be what I feel but it would put me in prison and I have no love of small, closed places. And some couples may celebrate an approaching divorce with a farewell tumble between the sheets but when I become that desperate for a woman I will become celibate,' he spelt out with brutal candour.

Humiliation pierced her like a knife-point. A primitive need to claw him for that unnecessary taunt charged her but a moment later she wanted to curl up and die. The condemned woman, branded a failure, finally scorned and cast aside. 'I hate you,' she framed strickenly.

'Then it is more than you felt for me before. Even hatred—it is something. There is hope for you yet,' he responded unfeelingly. 'Who was the man you were with?'

She spun away, savaged by him as she had been so often before. Only this time she was tormentingly aware that she was betraying her reactions and Rafael was receiving a vulture's satisfaction from her apparent new vulnerability. Her composure had cracked wide open earlier tonight. Now she was bare, stripped of all poise. 'Why should you want to know?'

'It amuses me to ask. It is so liberated to ask such a question of one's wife.' Provocation quivered through every accented syllable. 'Though perhaps not in your case. Hell will freeze over before you invite him into your bed!'

Outraged by his derision, she swung back. 'Are you so sure?'

Rafael stilled, straight ebony brows lowering over piercing tawny eyes.

'You and your bloody ego!' she gasped. 'Yes! That idea really gets to you, doesn't it? You can let some trollop crawl all over you six feet from me but——'

'Trollop?'

'Puta!' she spat, her emotions spinning into a fierce spiral of rage and mortification.

'No es,' Rafael fielded smoothly. 'I have never had to stoop to payment, *muñeca mia.*'

'Don't call me that!' she shrieked at him. 'I am not a doll!'

As he tilted his head to one side, his whole concentration unnervingly pinned to her, light glistened over the black silk luxuriance of his gleaming hair. 'You are arguing with me. *Increíble.* You are answering back,' he breathed in wonderment. 'You are even shouting.'

His response drained the wild, unfamiliar anger from her, leaving her weak and badly shaken up. 'Please go,' she whispered.

'Who taught you to shout?' he prompted. 'It is a very healthy sign. I like it.'

Her hands flew up, covering her ears. 'You are driving me out of my mind!'

'That is what you did to me. You threw my heart back at my feet and trampled on it. Two years of torture on this earth,' Rafael intoned rawly, his sensual mouth compressed into a white line. 'I gave you everything. You gave me nothing. You had the generosity of a miser. No woman has ever done to me what you dared to do. *Por dios,* when I think of how I suffered, I marvel that I stand here now and keep my hands from you...'

Involuntarily a hollow laugh escaped her. 'The sole saving grace of your visit is that you now possess that capability.'

Dark colour scorched his high cheekbones. 'You throw that in my teeth?'

She knew that intonation. Her tongue moistened her dry lips. It was the untrustworthy quiet before the storm.

'You think I made unnatural demands of you?' he raked at her between clenched teeth. 'Every time I touched you, I was made to feel like an animal. You lay like a block of ice beneath me, tolerating my filthy desires!'

Sarah was the one reddening now, spinning away to present him with a defensive back. 'Do you have to be so crude?'

He vented a stifled expletive. 'You are the only woman who has ever called me this...that,' he corrected in a driven undertone. 'To think that I was once enslaved by you...it makes me shudder.'

'The feeling *is* mutual.' Waves of pain were tearing at her. Rafael had not lost his impassioned powers of picturesque speech.

'Crude,' he repeated again.

Sarah went white, strangely ashamed of herself. On some crazy level she was attuned to the awareness that she had drawn real blood. A lean hand was clenched into a fist at the insult. Her eyes stung. He had never been crude. Indeed, for someone afflicted with his hot-blooded, over-sexed temperament, he had been extraordinarily gentle and patient and kind. Only it hadn't helped. Her inhibitions had proved insurmountable.

Sex. Just a small thing, not of great importance, something she could endure when she had to as no doubt other women had endured from the beginning of time. The sheer stupidity of her reasoning before their marriage tormented her now. Then she had been secretly flattered by the intensity of the hunger she roused in Rafael. Afterwards she had learnt to be afraid of that hunger, jerking away at his slightest touch.

It was typical of Rafael to be so gloriously and unashamedly wrapped up in his own sufferings, as he called them, she thought bitterly. Had he ever really thought of what it was like for her? To be married to a male so extravagantly gorgeous and innately virile and know you were a disaster in his bed? To live day in, day out with the knowledge that you were losing a little more of him by the hour? And finally to sink so low in a sense of utter inadequacy that she had taken his infidelity for granted. Closing her eyes, refusing to see. Anything just to keep him, anything so long as he stayed, a lesson learnt well at her mother's knee with a father whose extra-marital affairs were as numerous as they were well known.

Rafael was splashing brandy into a glass, throwing it back. Strong muscles worked in his brown throat. 'Tonight I will get drunk.'

'Are you driving?' The question fled her strained lips, inspired by an instinctive practicality and concern.

He shot her a gleaming, killing glance. 'So prosaic, so sensible, so much the lady. Your hair up like a royal princess, the not too revealing dress. This is what I lived with. The patronising smiles, the small talk when our marriage was dying. We must not notice. We must not talk about these personal, private things. It is not nice. That is the word.'

She was trembling. Oh, dear God, why had he had to come here to destroy her all over again? Look forward, never back, her great-aunt Letitia had once told her. Until now it had been excellent advice. Without Letitia's brusque and unsentimental support, Sarah wasn't entirely sure that she would have been here today, a completely different Sarah from the mixed-up, desperately unhappy girl she had been in her teens. She had come through a baptism of fire to find her own security. She no longer endured agonies of guilt over her parents' emotional blackmail. She no longer attempted to twist herself into something that she wasn't to please other people. In the year since she had made her home in London, Sarah had gone from strength to strength. But now, all of a sudden...horrifyingly, it was as though she had been catapulted back in time.

Why was Rafael behaving as if he were the innocent party? Innocence had deserted Rafael in his cradle. But conversely an image of him on a hot, dusty pavement laughingly bestowing flowers on a Parisienne baglady chose to surface in her mind's eye. Rafael, exuberantly, indescribably happy and wanting to share it with the world. In those days there had still been a streak of the child in Rafael. And now it was gone.

Hard cynicism curved his chiselled mouth. Nobody could stare like Rafael. You got the feeling that he could see right into you, strip away the concealing layers and pretences until only the inner self remained. 'Shall I call a taxi?' She couldn't bear the silence any longer.

'When I wish to leave, I will leave.' He loosed a hard, humourless laugh. 'I know why I am here. You will think me quite the sentimentalist. But I have this one question and it is not at all...nice.'

'I'd sooner not hear it, then.'

An ebony brow arched and she was suddenly, shockingly aware of the raw tension in his lean, powerful body. 'But you will,' he asserted fiercely. 'Did you ever regret it?'

'Regret what?'

Something akin to naked violence seethed in his brooding gaze, setting up tiny ripples of fear in the pulsing atmosphere. 'The price of family forgiveness. Is that how you thought of it?' he slung at her harshly. 'If God has given you a night of uninterrupted sleep in five years, he has been too good to you!'

In bewilderment, she muttered, 'What are you talking about?'

'You know what I am saying,' he bit out, if it was possible with even greater ferocity. 'Did it mean so little to you? A brief stay in some discreet clinic where I couldn't find you? It was against the law...it must have been somewhere very expensive. But what is expense to your parents when they find it within their power to destroy the last evidence of your most unfortunate marriage? Ah . . . you go pale. Did you think I would have forgotten so easily? How could I forget? It was an act of revenge. You did it to punish me!'

'Rafael, I——' she began, lost in the welter of demands that she didn't understand.

'You murdered my unborn child and I curse you for it. You did not have the right to make that choice. I will never forgive this nor will I ever forget it,' he swore in implacable condemnation. 'You did not want my child but I would have taken him, I would have brought him up . . .'

Sarah's perception of reality was rocking on its axis. A tiny sound dragged her glazed eyes from Rafael. Gilly was peering round the door, her pixie face screwed up against the intrusion of the light. She came stumbling across the room, powered by sudden noisy sobs. 'Ben tol' me the spider's gonna get me and eat me up!' she wailed, clutching at Sarah's skirt. 'And it was in my dream. Mummy, make it go away or give it to Ben. It's his spider!'

Rafael mumbled something incomprehensible in Spanish.

Sarah bent down to lift her daughter, smoothing a hand over her tousled black curls. Gilly pressed her face into her mother's shoulder. 'Who's dat man?'

'Never mind.' Curving protective arms tightly round Gilly's hot little body, she attempted to brush past Rafael.

A bruising set of fingers closed over her shoulder. 'She called you Mama. Who does she belong to? *Es imposible*. Speak!' he pressed fiercely.

Tearing free of his punishing hold, Sarah sped into the hall. Her sole concern was Gilly. Gilly must not be exposed to Rafael. She'd sink a knife between his ribs before she'd let him come within twenty feet of either of her children! He had accused her of aborting their child. Of course, he couldn't believe that! A piece of nonsense, that was what it was! Some sly, sneaky gambit aimed at explaining away a four-year uninterest in fatherhood? He must think she was mentally deficient. Well, she wasn't and where her children were concerned she would fight like a lioness. Had natural curiosity finally pierced his tough hide? Well, it was too late. He was nearly five years too late. He wasn't walking in here now to exercise rights he had surrendered of his own free will . . . no way was he doing that!

Her hands were shaking so violently that she had trouble in covering Gilly up again. Her daughter was much too sleepy to notice the state she was in. 'Is it gone away?' she mumbled.

'Far, far away,' Sarah soothed tremulously, scanning the other single bed with frightened eyes. Ben was just a bump under the duvet, not a centimetre of him in sight. In sleep, Ben was a burrower. Gilly was a sprawler, kicking the bedding off while she slept.

Rafael was blocking her exit from the bedroom. She raised her hands. 'You can't come in here.'

He wasn't moving anywhere. Neither forward nor back. 'Madre de Dios,' he muttered weakly, lapsing into Spanish, accented syllables rising and falling disjointedly.

Her palms planted against his broad chest. She thrust him bodily from the room, hauling the door closed behind her, denying him even the view. In none of these instinctive reactions did she recognise herself. Fear and rage were consuming her in equal parts. 'Go!' she gasped. 'I don't want you here!'

A brown hand collided abruptly with her shoulder, forcing her back to the wall. 'My daughter . . . she's got black hair. She has to be mine. She has to be!' he grated.

'Not yours. Not unless you can call basic biology paternity!'

Hooded tiger's eyes bore down on her. 'And the other one?'

'Twins!' she snapped.

A flaring, incredulous fury had entered his dark features. Before she could retreat, he slammed a hand to the wall an inch or two from her ear. The reverbation tremored through her pounding temples. He frightened her half out of her wits. 'So you lied to me. All of you lied! The abortion story? A lie. *Por dios,* a lie!' he vented in the soaring crescendo of all-encompassing black fury. 'All this time, all these years a lie to enable you to steal my children from me. You think you can do this with impunity? You think I would let a frozen vixen raise my own flesh and blood? For this you will pay. You will lose them. I will take them away.'

Sarah was beyond understanding a tithe of what was happening to her. She grasped only that final, searing threat. 'You can't do that!'

He withdrew his hands. 'I will see you and your family in court. I have papers. There is no reference to my children. I have proof of what has been done to me. No judge will award custody to a woman who is both a liar and a cheat!'

Sarah gazed at him in horror. He wasn't even looking at her. He was heading out of the door. She raced after him, heedless of her bare feet. In panic she clutched at the sleeve of his jacket and he shook her off in violent repudiation. 'Liar!' he roared at her loud enough to wake the entire building.

But still she skidded in his wake. The instinct to pursue was her only driving purpose. When the lift doors slotted closed, she fled down the stairs two at a time, round and round and round again until she charged dizzily across the small, polished foyer.

'Mrs Southcott!' The security man exclaimed, jumping out of his seat to follow her.

A black Lamborghini raked off down the street with the speed of a jet on a runway. Sarah stood in the centre of the pavement, strands of pale hair falling round her fevered cheeks.

'What happened?'

Dumbly she faced the anxious guard, not at all sure what she was doing outside in the evening air. 'Nothing...nothing,' she said again.

Shivering, she stepped into the lift. Angela's mother was standing at her flat door, peering in. 'I heard someone shouting. My goodness, you look dreadful! My dear,' she gushed.

'I'm sorry if you were disturbed.' Sarah backed hurriedly into her own flat and shut the door.

How had her tranquil world suddenly exploded into a nightmare? Rafael had uttered insane threats. Why had she panicked? But questions without viable answers were circulating in her spinning head. Rafael did not tell lies. Not even social lies. In times gone by he had used blunt candour as a weapon against her parents, watching them reel in civilised shock from the stinging bite of unapologetic honesty.

A monstrous suspicion was growing in her mind. She relived Rafael's shattered response to Gilly's appearance, his floundering speech...his silence. She remembered the documents she had signed unread almost five years ago. I have proof, Rafael had hurled in challenge. And if that was true, it meant that her father had deliberately concealed the twins' birth by ensuring that no mention of them appeared on paper. That thought plunged her into a black hole and spawned other thoughts that brought her out in a cold sweat of fear.

Had Rafael ever received her letter? No matter what her father had done, she had still had faith in her mother. What choice had she had? When you were ill, you were dependent on others. A damp chill enclosed her body. Tomorrow she would have to tackle her parents. There had to be some reasonable explanation, there just had to be. Somewhere along the line a misunderstanding had occurred and Rafael had been the victim. But as she lay sleepless in her bed, her mind revolving in frantic, frightened circles, she failed to see just how such a gross misinterpretation of past events could innocently have taken place.

And try as she might she could not help but remember that fateful three weeks in Paris. A tide of colourful, unforgettable impressions was surging back to her. The intriguing bookstalls on the corner of the Pont au Double; the evocative scent of the mauve blossoms weighting the empress trees on the Rue de Furstenberg; the dazzling array of fresh fruit and vegetables at the Mouffetard market; the sinfully sweet taste of Tunisian honey cakes from the Rue de la Huchette...

In her final year at school, she had been lonely and isolated, too quick to grasp at any overture of friendship. She had blocked out the awareness that her classmates thought Margo a spiteful, unpleasant girl. Margo's invitation had been a much-needed confidence booster, her subsequent behaviour a painful slap on the face.

Margo had invited her to Paris solely to please her widowed father. On the day of her arrival, the other girl had made it resentfully obvious that Sarah would not have been her choice of a holiday companion.

'Dad thinks you'll cramp my style but he's wrong,' Margo had asserted sullenly. 'I have a boyfriend at the Sorbonne. I've got better things to do with my time than trail you around like a third wheel!'

She should have flown home again but she had had too much pride. Having pleaded with her parents to let her accept the invitation, she had shrunk from admitting that she had made a mistake. Margo's father had been a successful businessman, very rarely at home and far too busy to concern himself with her entertainment. He had assumed that his daughter was showing her guest round Paris. It had not occurred to him that Sarah might be left to show herself around.

She had been free as a bird for the very first time in her life. Nobody had had the slightest interest in where she went or what she did. Venturing out with a very boring guidebook, she had been intimidated by the seething anonymity of the crowds and the incredible traffic. On the third day, while she was standing at a busy intersection trying to make sense of a map, disaster had struck. A youth on a motorbike had whizzed past at speed, snatching her shoulder-bag and sending her sprawling into the gutter. Rafael had come to her assistance.

In that split second, the entire course of her future had changed. He had helped her to her feet, asking her in fluent French if she was hurt. He had switched to equally polished English in receipt of her stammering attempts to express herself in a foreign language. She had looked up into dark golden eyes in an arrestingly handsome face and time had stood still. When the clock started ticking again, everything had undergone a subtle transformation. The sun had been brighter, the crowds less stifling, and the loss of her bag had inexplicably become an annoying irritation rather than an over-whelming tragedy.

Do you believe in love at first sight? she had once been tempted to ask Karen, only she had been very much afraid that Karen would laugh. But something reckless and exhilarating and frightening had seized hold of her in that instant.

Meeting Rafael had been like colliding with a meteor and falling back into bottomless space, completely dazed by the experience. Louise Southcott's daughter, who was very careful never to speak to strangers, had let herself be picked up in the street and in a terrifyingly short space of time Rafael had become the centre of her universe.

'You're so quiet...so mysterious,' he had once teased, running a long finger caressingly across her lips, smiling when she skittishly pulled her head back. He had never doubted his ability to awaken her to an answering sensuality when he so desired.

But then Rafael had not seen a desperately insecure teenager. He had seen a young woman, expensively clothed, her features matured by expertly applied cosmetics. Superficially, she had possessed considerable poise. Rafael had fallen in love with her face, the face that he had been unable to capture to his own satisfaction on canvas.

And Sarah? Sarah had been drawn, entrapped and finally mesmerised by his emotional intensity. Passion was the mainspring of Rafael's volatile temperament. He loved with passion, he created hauntingly beautiful works of art with passion and, she realised now on a tide of pain and regret, he hated with passion as well...

'Who was dat man?' Gilly asked sullenly over breakfast.

'What man?' Sarah muttered evasively.

Gilly frowned. 'That man,' she said louder.

'What man?' Ben picked up the refrain.

Sarah stood up, sliding her untouched toast surreptitiously into the bin. 'He was someone I met at the party last night.'

'You look funny, Mummy,' Ben said thoughtfully.

'Funny Mummy,' Gilly rhymed and giggled, as ever mercurial in her moods.

She phoned Angela and asked if she would babysit for her again. Since Sarah paid well, the teenager was more than willing to oblige. But naturally she was surprised. On Saturdays, Sarah always took the children to see their grandparents. It was an arrangement that was religiously observed but not one, Sarah reflected, that was of any real satisfaction to any of them. Her parents complained bitterly about the small amount of time she allowed them to spend with their grandchildren and Sarah always found the visits a strain. The twins had all the boundless exuberance and vitality of their father. Within an hour of their arrival, little looks would be exchanged by her parents, cold criticisms of her methods of child-rearing uttered, and the twins would go horribly quiet as the atmosphere became repressive and disapproving.

It was a bright beautiful morning with clear skies and sunlight. The promise of early summer was in the air. Normally she enjoyed the drive to Southcott Lodge. She rarely used her car except at weekends. It had belonged to her great-aunt and, having been well maintained, was mercifully still going strong in spite of its age. When the car did develop problems, she doubted that she would be able to replace it.

Inflation had considerably reduced the value of the income she received from a small trust fund set up by her late grandmother. Five mornings a week she worked as a receptionist in a large insurance company while the twins were at nursery school. The flat was her one asset and already it was becoming cramped.

Her family home was an elegant red-brick Georgian house set in spacious, landscaped grounds. Even the lawns looked manicured. The exterior was as picture perfect as the interior. The innate tidiness of her parents' lives was matched by their surroundings.

The housekeeper, Mrs Purbeck, opened the front door. Her brow creased as she noted the absence of the twins. 'Your parents are in the conservatory, Miss Southcott.'

'Thank you, Mrs Purbeck.' Sarah crushed back a ludicrous desire to laugh. On Saturdays, in spring and summer, her parents always breakfasted in the conservatory. Her father would be reading his morning paper at one end of the table and at the other her mother would be staring into space. Neither would find it necessary to speak to the other unless something of importance arose.

'Sarah...you're early.' Folding his paper into precise folds, Charles Southcott rose to his feet, a tall, distinguished man in his late fifties, his blond hair greying, his eyes ice-blue chips of enquiry in his long, thin face.

Her mother frowned. 'Where are the children?'

Sarah took a deep breath. 'I haven't brought them.'

An anxious pleat-line formed between Louise's pencilled brows.

'You see, I needed to talk to you privately,' Sarah confided tensely.

Her father appraised her pale face and taut stance. 'Is there something wrong, Sarah? Sit down and we'll talk about it calmly.' Although she had yet to do or say anything that was not calm, there was a cold note of warning to the command.

Sarah swallowed hard. 'I saw Rafael last night.'

Her mother turned a ghastly shade beneath her well-applied make-up. Her father was not so easily read. He continued to watch her without visible reaction. The silence threatened to strangle Sarah, forcing her to keep on talking. 'Gordon took me to a party and he was there.'

'What sort of people are you mixing with these days?' Louise's voice betrayed the shaky undertones of stress.

'Afterwards, he came to the apartment.'

Charles Southcott showed his first response in a chilling narrowing of his gaze. 'At your invitation?'

Her mother looked at him with reproach. 'Sarah wouldn't have invited him into her home.'

'He didn't know about the twins,' Sarah advanced stiffly. 'He said that he thought I...I had had a termination. He said that that was what he was told.'

A dragging quiet lay over the room. Louise studied her clasped hands, still as a statue. Her father's features were shuttered, a tiny nerve pulling at the edge of his flattened mouth.

'I mean...that's just so ridiculous.' Sarah was wretchedly conscious of the high-pitched note that had entered her voice.

Charles Southcott expelled his breath shortly. 'Sit down, Sarah. We don't want a scene.'

She was feeling sick, shaky. Facing up to her father still had that effect on her. She sank down reluctantly into an elaborately cushioned wickerwork chair, her back a ramrod-straight rejection of its comfortable embrace.

'Let me make one point clear in advance. We were solely responsible for your welfare,' her father delivered with an air of strong censure. 'When Alejandro went to New York and left you here with us, we were extremely concerned about you. Your marriage was destroying you.'

'He was destroying her,' her mother chipped in, tight-mouthed with bitterness. 'He turned you into a stranger. We lost you and you never came back to us.'

Sarah's throat was closing over, hurting her. 'He was my husband and I loved him.'

Charles Southcott released a cutting laugh. 'You didn't love him, Sarah. You were obsessed by him. It was a sick obsession and you needed help...'

'Help?' Sarah repeated chokily. 'You call locking me up helping me?'

'Sarah,' Louise whispered pleadingly. 'Please...'

'It was for your own good. I didn't want to hurt you. I wanted to bring you to your senses,' her father continued coldly. 'When Alejandro had the impertinence to show up here again...'

Sarah froze. 'Rafael came here?' she prompted in disbelief.

Her mother murmured, 'We had to keep him away from you, Sarah. You weren't well. You might have had a miscarriage. We didn't really lie to him. He jumped to conclusions and we didn't contradict him.'

An unpleasant smile that was no smile at all had formed on her father's narrow mouth. 'I believe it's relatively common for Latins to believe that sin is inevitably followed by some holy form of retribution,' he scoffed. 'I confirmed his suspicions.'

Sarah was leaning dizzily forward. 'Oh, dear God, how could you do that to him?' she gasped in horror.

'Naturally I saw that the letter you intended to send was destroyed,' he added icily. 'While it was unhappily not within my power to prevent you from making a fool of yourself over him for two years, it was within my power to prevent you from doing so on paper.'

Sarah shuddered under the lash of his contempt.

'I loved him,' she whispered abstractedly. 'And at the beginning I trusted you. He blames me and he's right to blame me,' she vented with a shaken gasp. 'Nobody has any excuse to be that naïve. You made me believe that he had just cut me out of his life as if I didn't exist. You didn't care what that did to me. But then you didn't care what you did to me by putting me in that place . . .'

'It was our duty to protect you from yourself.'

'You took your chance when I was in no fit state to know what you were doing,' Sarah condemned. 'You hadn't been able to buy him off. You hadn't been able to scare him off. So you lied to him and you lied to me and nothing you can say will change those facts!'

'Why are we arguing about something that was finished most conclusively five years ago?' Charles Southcott surveyed her with sharp distaste. 'I did you a favour. You were well rid of him.'

Sarah sprang upright on a wild surge of anger. 'What did you know about our marriage? Did it ever occur to you that I wasn't the perfect wife? Why did you assume that I was such a precious gift?' she demanded strickenly. 'And at least Rafael didn't treat me the way you treat my mother!'

She dashed a trembling hand across her streaming eyes. Until that moment she hadn't realised that she was crying. The silence was so familiar, chilling, suffocating. 'I should have known,' she framed tremulously, defying the icy silence to the last. 'I should have known.'

She walked out and they let her go as she had known they would. They would give her time to calm down and in a few days they would approach her, expecting family loyalty to have haltered her out-of-control emotions. Only this time that wouldn't happen. Sarah only visited for her mother's sake. She had always made excuses for her mother but now she had to face the fact that Louise had been in full collusion and agreement with her husband and she was nauseated by the knowledge that her parents had deliberately set out to break up her marriage and continued to rejoice in their success. Neither of them was remotely concerned about the high costs she had had to pay five years ago.

She sat in her car in the driveway for several dazed minutes. Her brain was roving off in a dozen different directions until it abruptly settled on one overwhelming necessity, a thread of seeming sanity in the nightmare of confusion. She had to find out where Rafael was staying. She had to see him, speak to him.

Karen answered her phone with a grumbling yawn. 'Sarah,' she muttered. 'Why are you using a callbox?'

'Do you know where Rafael Alejandro is staying?' In the lengthy quiet that settled on the line, Sarah regretted her impetuosity and improvised awkwardly, 'Someone I know needs to get in touch with him urgently.'

'And you need to see a man about a dog.' Karen was suddenly sounding very alert. 'Actually I do know. Elise let it drop last night in a temper.'

'Elise?'

'The lady who brought him. Or should I say, the lady he allowed to bring him?' Karen extended with irony. 'I think we need a trade-off here, Sarah, my pet. Information for information.'

'Karen, please!' Sarah said impatiently.

Karen surrendered with bad grace and supplied the address.

'Thanks. Thanks!' Sarah said again. 'I'll be in touch.'

It was a small but exclusive apartment block in Belgravia. Pushing a nervous hand through the damp hair adhering to her forehead, Sarah stepped into the lift. She felt hot and bothered, utterly bereft of her usual cool. A little belatedly, she was wondering what she intended to say to Rafael and whether, in the heat of the moment, she might have been too hasty in her urge to immediately seek him out. She flinched when the lift doors whirred back and then she walked uncertainly along a corridor floored with a soft, deep carpet. The nasty suspicion that she might be about to make a gigantic fool of herself increased her reluctance.

A vase of beautifully arranged flowers sat in an alcove to one side of the entrance. Did Rafael own this place? Rent it? Whichever, this luxury was a far cry from the sort of flats they had once shared. She smoothed moist palms down over the tailored navy jacket and straight skirt she wore. Rafael hated navy. Frowning at the irrelevancy that her subconscious had served up, she pressed the bell.

She was midway through a second prolonged ring when the door jerked wide, framing Rafael. He was in the act of donning a white silk shirt, his thick hair damp and tousled from the shower. Drops of crystalline moisture still glistened on the wealth of black curling hair hazing his muscular chest. Involuntarily Sarah averted her eyes from the endless expanse of lean, golden flesh on view. Dry-mouthed, she swallowed. An odd tingling sensation ran down her backbone before she forced her head up again.

Raking golden eyes skimmed over her taut face and the brilliance of the unconscious appeal in her amethyst gaze. His superb bone-structure hardened, his ruthlessly sensual mouth tightening. Sensual...yes, those clean sculpted lines belied by that wholly passionate curve were uniquely sensual. The obscure thought-train surged up on Sarah out of nowhere, shocking her, sending rebellious heat to warm her skin. Her chaotic responses smashed her concentration and she was further confused by his silence. Silence from Rafael was an unknown quantity that unnerved her.

'I need to talk to you.' It emerged more as a plea than as the adult acknowledgement she had intended.

He took a fluid step back, employing body language to concede agreement. But it was a grudging invitation. He didn't have to speak to tell her that. Rafael could put out vibes like placards. She was acutely conscious of the burning hostility he emanated.

'I'm going out in ten minutes.' Neither apology nor warning sounded in his intonation. It was an assertion that, no matter what she did, no matter what she said, he had no real intention of listening to her.

'Perhaps you'll change your mind when you hear what I have to say,' Sarah fenced daringly.

CHAPTER THREE

SARAH was shown into a spacious lounge. It was very untidy. Books lay open on the couch. Cushions were tumbled on the floor and empty glasses littered a fine antique occasional table. And, oddly enough, for a timeless moment Sarah felt more at home and less of an intruder. The chaos which Rafael wreaked on his surroundings was disturbingly familiar and it threw up memories that threatened her self-discipline.

'You have six minutes left,' Rafael said with flaring impatience.

Sarah collided with intent golden eyes and hurriedly looked away again, her breath catching in her throat. 'I saw my parents this morning.'

His strong jawline hardened. 'Surely not an unusual event?' he jibed. 'Even when we were living in Paris, you contrived to see them three weeks out of every four!'

Her colour heightened but she decided to ignore the taunt. 'Until I spoke to them, I had no idea that you returned to England to see me five years ago. Please believe that. They didn't tell me.'

His narrowed hawk-like stare was discouraging. He exuded a daunting indifference to the revelation she had made. 'That I can believe,' he conceded unexpectedly. 'What I do not comprehend is what this has to do with the present.'

Her emotions were running perilously close to the surface. Rigid with strain, she looked at him in stark appeal. 'Don't you understand? If... if I'd known, I would have been there...'

47

'De veras?' Rafael spread eloquent hands wide in a gesture of disbelief. 'To greet your adulterous husband with open arms?'

Sarah visibly flinched from the suggestion.

Rafael arched a jet brow, his golden appraisal brilliant with contempt. 'I think not.'

'Since the situation didn't arise, I can't say what would have happened. But I would never have lied to you about the twins! Rafael...' Her tongue tripped clumsily over the syllables. There was so much she needed to tell him but it was incredibly difficult to find the right words. To be open and honest about past events with so little encouragement demanded a degree of bravado that she had not previously exercised in Rafael's radius. Frustration ran through her like a current. Self-expression was Rafael's talent, not hers. Nobody ever went in ignorance of how Rafael felt or what he wanted and that ability, she appreciated now, was no small advantage in life. 'You must see that this isn't easy for——'

'Have you had breakfast yet? Lord, I'm sorry!' From somewhere above them another voice had intervened. 'I was in the shower and I thought it was the television I was hearing! I didn't realise you had someone here.'

A breathtaking Scandinavian blonde with wheat-gold hair streaming over her towelling-clad shoulders was looking down at them from the gallery that overlooked the lounge. Sarah stared up at her, silenced, transfixed, every vestige of colour fleeing her complexion. Ludicrous as it seemed to her, the blonde wore a friendly smile of apology which slowly changed into an anxious frown as she skimmed a questioning glance at Rafael before disappearing from sight.

Shock always made Sarah go cold. A clammy chill was enclosing her flesh in a shuddering embrace. With the cold had come an unwelcome return to sanity. What madness had driven her into coming here? A woman in a time-warp had enacted the last few frantic hours. Had she once paused to think rationally about what she was doing? No, she hadn't. She had recklessly run Rafael to earth and what she had sown, she had reaped. Her sense of humiliation was choking. Shame burnt like ice through her veins. With what fantasies had she rushed here five years too late? The glowing, utterly unselfconscious blonde on the gallery had recalled everything that Sarah had worked so hard to forget.

Once Rafael had held her trapped in a silken web more powerful than the strongest steel. And she had lost all self-will. That was what loving somebody like Rafael did to you. Perhaps she should be grateful to her father, she thought feverishly. Perhaps she should be thanking him for her freedom. He had torn her from that web and forced her to survive without Rafael.

She had thought that what she refused to acknowledge couldn't hurt her. But in the end her fearful blindness had ripped her to shreds. While Rafael was in New York, her father had put a private investigator on him. Her father had turned her shrinking suspicions into cold, irrefutable fact. He had framed Rafael's infidelity in black and white typescript and enshrined it in the unforgettable images of a photograph. He had brought her face to face with the living substance of her worst nightmares. And in expecting gratitude, her father had demanded the impossible from her.

'Sarah...'

She forced a frozen smile on to lips that for a frightening instant felt too clumsy to obey her. Loathing was emerging from that terrible chilled feeling deep down inside her. Loathing and embarrassment and seething anger were ready to thrust a violent passage through her controlled façade. Their marriage was over, past, dead...something she had briefly allowed herself to forget. Quite *how* she could have forgotten that reality evaded her understanding.

'Sarah...' Ironically, Rafael was now regarding her with the full attention he had earlier been determined to deny her. His penetrating gaze rested on her with unnerving intensity. 'Presumably you did come here to tell me something,' he reasoned with a patience that was quite out of character.

'Did I?' Her mind was a terrifying blank when it came to sane, civilised responses. Indeed all of a sudden she didn't know what she was doing here in his apartment. 'I thought you were in a hurry,' she said curtly.

'I feel in less of a hurry,' Rafael countered lazily. 'Why don't you sit down?'

Sarah clutched her envelope bag to her stomach in a white-knuckled grip that betrayed her mood better than any words would have. 'Because I don't feel like sitting down now.'

He slanted her a disarming smile. 'Before we were interrupted, you were about to tell me something,' he murmured in a coaxing, soothing tone.

'Was I?'

Rafael moved a beautifully expressive hand. It signified apology for his earlier brevity and indifference, indicated that he was now prepared to be a captive audience. It was marvellous what Rafael could put into one casual gesture. He was poetry in motion, poetry even standing still. In absolute anguish at the rebellious trend of her muddled brain, Sarah stiffened even more.

'I will give you my time, all the time that you want,' he proffered with quite unintentional arrogance. 'I will be quiet. I will not interrupt as I did before. I will listen to what you want to say.'

Yes, she thought sickly...yes, how he would have revelled in hearing what she might have foolishly confessed had not the blonde interrupted them. Five years ago, had circumstances been otherwise, had her father not committed one final, unforgivable act in his determination to destroy her marriage, she would have been at Southcott Lodge when Rafael arrived.

Her father utterly intimidated most people. But not Rafael. Challenged, Rafael could assume an icy, chilling dignity more than equal to anything her father could produce. Sarah had long understood that it was for that reason that she had been forcibly removed from the scene. She had been the weak link in the chain and her father had broken her as he had not been able to break Rafael.

Given the opportunity, Rafael would have told her the truth about that woman in New York. He would have made no excuses for himself. She would have sat there not looking at him and trying very hard not to listen. He would have been perfectly capable of flinging himself at her feet and pleading for forgiveness without losing an ounce of his fierce pride.

And she would have gone back to him. Why? Simply because she loved him, loved him the way she had never dreamt she could ever love anybody, loved him the way she never, ever wanted to love anybody again. A shudder of repulsion ran through her. Thank God, she had been deprived of that choice. Rafael would have managed to convince her that that woman in New York had only been an isolated episode, much regretted and never to be repeated. At nineteen, she had been very naïve, very impressionable and Rafael had considerable powers of persuasion.

Lifting her small head high, Sarah cleared her throat. 'The twins——'

Rafael broke his vow of silence. 'The twins?' he interrupted as though he had been expecting her to refer to something entirely different.

'They're happy, well-adjusted children,' Sarah completed. 'They don't need an occasional father. And I sincerely doubt that a pair of curious four-year-olds on scene would facilitate what appears to be a hectic sexual calendar.'

'Ah.' Rafael continued to regard her with infuriating cool. 'And on what do you base this assumption?'

'In little more than twelve hours, I have seen you with two different women!' Sarah stressed thinly, holding on to her temper with difficulty.

'There is something strange about this?' Rafael queried, gently ironic.

'If you think that I intend to expose my children to your immorality, you are very much mistaken!' Sarah told him hotly, flags of pink highlighting her cheekbones. 'I insist that you stay out of our lives!'

Rafael inclined his dark head. 'Or is it that you wish to insist that I stay out of other beds?' he prompted, silky soft, his eyes gleaming rapiers on her flushed features.

Sarah blinked, completely thrown by the enquiry. 'I beg your pardon?'

'Indeed you might,' he riposted. 'But I am prepared to dispense with the apology. This conversation . . . it has immense entertainment value.'

'I don't know what you're talking about!' Sarah snapped frustratedly. 'I'm not going to apologise for stating my views.'

'Your views are most unnatural for a woman who has been separated from her husband for five years by her own choice.'

For several tense seconds, Sarah ruminated fiercely over that incomprehensible response. 'Unnatural?' she repeated sharply. 'I intend to protect the twins from your influence.'

'But who is to protect them from yours and that of your parents?' Rafael asked with devastating derision. 'I would not in conscience permit one of you to raise a hamster in captivity.'

'How dare you say that to me?' Sarah was outraged by the insult.

Before she could stalk past him, he shot out a long-fingered hand and enclosed her slim forearm in a grip of iron. 'How...dare...I?' he demanded in a raw, incredulous undertone, an outrage a hundredfold greater than her own blazing in the extraordinary depths of his tiger's eyes. 'Had I less self-control, I would show you how I feel. You have denied me my children. I have lost four irreplaceable years of their lives. I am their father and I am a stranger to them. They could walk past me in the street and I wouldn't know them. I don't even know their names! For what you have selfishly stolen from me and from them, I could quite happily kill you!'

In a movement of grim repudiation, he released her numbed arm and she reeled back from him, white and shaken, her knees trembling supports. 'I never dreamt that you didn't know about Gilly and Ben!' she protested weakly.

'You expect me to believe that?'

'I'm telling you the truth!'

He vented a harsh laugh, swinging lithely away from her. 'Do you think I do not know what brought you here?' he sliced back at her chillingly. 'You are afraid of what I can do.'

Sarah fixed her distraught gaze on his darkly handsome features in a mixture of fear and defiance. 'You can't do anything!'

His mouth curved into a hard, glittering smile. 'Sarah, in some matters you are still so naïve. You cannot have legal custody of the children. That can only be achieved by agreement between husband and wife or a judicial decision,' he pointed out. 'There has been no such agreement, no such decision. And should you oppose my claim, the lies and deception employed to keep me in ignorance of my children's very existence will scarcely help your case. In court, nothing will be concealed...'

A giant mailed fist was suddenly pounding a tattoo behind her temples. 'We...we don't have to go to court.' She had to force the words of appeasement past her bloodless lips. 'We...we could talk.'

'Talk? I have heard you talk.' Rafael dealt her a blistering look of condemnation. 'In the future if you desire to talk to anyone you may talk with my lawyer here in London. He may have more patience than I.'

He had mastered his anger and that frightened her more. In anger, Rafael could still be reached. 'I don't want to talk to your lawyer,' she muttered tightly.

Rafael swept a jacket off the couch and sent a flaring glance of impatience down at the thin gold watch on his wrist. 'This is sad. For you, not for me. Now, if you don't mind...?'

'All right, I'm going!' Sarah took the decided hint with moritified alacrity, hurrying out to the hall to let herself out of the apartment.

When Sarah was deeply upset, it was not unusual for her to take refuge in the mundane practicalities of everyday life. She wouldn't let herself think about Rafael's threats while she negotiated the traffic and recalled that she had not yet done the weekly shopping. So she hurtled busily into a crowded supermarket, raced up and down the aisles and ended up staring sightlessly into a freezer compartment before her defences gave way and the full horror of Rafael's confident threats about lawyers and courts and judicial decisions washed over her like a tidal wave.

She squeezed her eyes shut in a futile attempt to stem the tears flooding her eyes. She had not said what she'd intended to say. She had not said what she should have said. But on one count she had told him the whole truth. She could not face a future studded with flying visits from Rafael. Not when the mere sight of him with another woman still turned her into a seething cauldron of bitterness and defeat. Rafael was a cruel reminder of everything she did not want to remember. She should never have gone near him. Instead of pouring oil on troubled water, she had lit another torch.

He had already made several lightning-fast deductions. She did not have legal custody of the twins. Until Rafael had mentioned the fact, she had not even thought of the matter. Gilly and Ben had always been hers, solely hers. From the moment of their birth, they had been the centre...no, the entirety of her life. She had nothing else, had never wanted anything else, had never feared that anyone, least of all Rafael, might seek to take her children from her.

But what chance would she have in a court? In a court where 'nothing would be concealed'? Her blood ran cold. She had terrifying visions of Rafael dredging up the facts of her own unhappy childhood and the subsequent effect on her development and building on those facts to insinuate that she couldn't possibly be a good mother.

Nor would it stop there. Rafael didn't know everything. But he could find out, couldn't he? Wouldn't any good lawyer go digging to establish exactly where she had been and what she had been doing for every month of the past five years? Rafael had a whole barrage of weapons he had yet to discover. Beads of perspiration formed on her short upper lip. An emotion that was nothing short of sheer terror spread to the depth of an abyss inside her.

'Are you feeling all right, dear?'

Blankly she looked at the little old lady staring at her. From somewhere she dredged the self-possession to nod and force stiff legs onward in a semblance of normality. Dear God, she had nearly told all to Rafael in her urge to wipe the slate clean and establish her own innocence of duplicity. But had she confessed all, what a weapon she would have been giving him! He didn't think she was fit to bring up the twins as it was.

All the way back home, she made frantic, crazy plans to pack up lock, stock and barrel and disappear with the children into thin air. When fantasy ran out of fuel on the balance of her bank account, she came back down to earth. She had to talk Rafael out of taking her to court. That was the only alternative to flight, and since she had never managed to talk Rafael out of anything with the smallest degree of success she could not feel too hopeful of the outcome. Why should he listen to her now? It was a question she asked herself over and over again for the remainder of the day and the sleepless night that followed.

She slept in the next morning. Awakening she glanced at the clock and groaned. The twins had missed Sunday school and she couldn't possibly get dressed in time to take them to church. The day continued as it had begun. Lunch was a burnt offering and afterwards she decided to take Gilly and Ben to the park across the road from the flat.

They had only been there about ten minutes when the twins began fighting over a bucket in the sandpit. As Ben triumphed, Gilly lost her balance and fell. With a screech of temper, she sprang up again and threw her whole weight at her brother. Ben grabbed a handful of black, curling hair and yanked. A scream that would have wakened the dead erupted from Gilly.

Sarah waded in. 'Stop it!'

'I don't want your dirty ol' bucket!' Gilly shouted ferociously and raced off towards the swings.

Ben swiftly took off in the same direction. The bucket was forgotten. Now that his sister didn't want it any more, it had lost its appeal. Grimly conscious of the pitying and superior glances of two other mothers nearby, Sarah retreated to a bench. Even at a distance it was obvious that her children were enjoying a heated dispute over the one vacant swing. She heaved a guilty sigh of relief when another child abandoned a swing and

Ben took possession. Today the twins had been particularly argumentative and perhaps she was partly responsible, she reflected wryly. Nervous tension was making her feel like a novice tightrope walker and children were highly sensitive to atmosphere.

Glancing away from the twins, she caught sight of the tall, black-haired male standing beneath the trees some thirty yards from the swings. Tautening in alarm, she scrambled upright, made a jerky movement forward and then stilled again.

As much as Rafael's entire concentration was focused on Gilly and Ben, Sarah's was relentlessly bent on him. Somehow she could sense his raw frustration, his uncertainty of what to do next. It was there in the taut lines of his lean, powerful body, in the angle of his arrogant dark head and the silent jut of his jawline. Something poignant and unnameable in his chosen isolation tore at her heart and sent her barriers crashing down, forcing her to rise above the terrible, tortured confusion of her own emotions. Had he intended to come here? Or had he not been able to stay away? His shock over the discovery that he was a father had understandably been replaced by a burning desire for knowledge. Yet had there been any other children of the same age and colouring with the twins he might not have been able to identify them. Pain clenched her stomach muscles as he turned away and began heading for the exit without making any attempt to approach either her or the children.

Without thinking about it, Sarah found herself racing after him. She was within feet of him when he spun round fluidly to face her. The cold anger in his set dark features was a physical entity, powered by the bitter denunciation in his hard stare.

'*Por qué?*' he demanded of her and in that single phrase dwelt a wealth of judgement and bitterness. 'Why?'

Sarah paled. 'We have to talk.'

'Talk? Why should I talk to you now?' he flared. 'Did you talk to me when you decided you wanted out of our marriage? No. You hid behind your parents. You made your choice, Sarah. Now you have to live with it.'

'You gave me an ultimatum,' she reminded him in a hot surge of spirit. 'How many daughters are willing to cut off their parents and never see them again?'

'I didn't ask you to choose. I made the decision,' Rafael drawled with unflinching clarity. 'You were my wife. Your loyalty should have been to your husband.'

Angrily she threw her head back and challenged him. 'You simply expected me to obey you, didn't you?'

Apparently unaware of any inherent fault in such reasoning, Rafael surveyed her with all the fierce, uncompromising pride that was his strength. 'What else would I expect?' he turned the question boldly back on her. 'I knew what had to be done if our marriage was to survive. I chose the only course.'

'And you never had any doubt of that, did you?' Helpless sarcasm thickened her voice.

'Self-doubt is not a habit of mine. I stand by my decisions,' he delivered deflatingly.

'In the same way I suppose it never occurred to you that your responsibilities towards me might extend to more than one fleeting enquiry of my parents as to where I was?' Sarah retorted sharply.

Dark blood flamed over his high cheekbones, fury in the slashing line of his wide mouth. 'I believed you were ridding yourself of my child.'

'You were pretty quick to accept that, weren't you?' Her temper was rising steadily. 'It suited you to believe that. You were having a whale of a time in New York. Your exhibition was a sell-out to rave reviews. Maybe my parents were right about you all along...' Raggedly she paused for breath.

'I may thank God that we parted before you hurled lines of that nature,' Rafael slotted in with biting satire.

'I expect you do. When you were broke, I was money in the bank. When you weren't, I was a liability and a pregnant liability at that!' Sarah condemned in a furious rush of emotion.

'Eso basta!' Rafael gritted in an incensed undertone. 'You think a public park is the place for this?'

Sarah froze, cast a scurrying and anxious glance to either side and established to her own satisfaction that the trees concealed them from general view. 'If it doesn't bother me, why should it bother you?' she slung, growing in stature. 'You can't blame me for everything that went wrong!'

His jawline clenched. 'Can you not speak the truth even now? Why did you marry me?'

'I...I was unfortunate enough to fall in love with you.' Cornered into the grudging admission, she felt as though she had lost valuable ground.

'Whose delusion is that?' he derided. 'It has never been mine. Let me refresh your memory. You were desperate to escape your parents but you didn't have the guts to rebel on your own. You needed me to fight them for you. And when you had made your escape and found the big wide world less to your taste than you had anticipated, you realised that Mama and Papa could be brought to their knees if you hung out long enough. Once you had them there, you graciously agreed to return to the fold...'

'It wasn't like that; it was never like that!'

Stinging contempt glittered in his intent gaze. 'What a shame that you neglected to tell me that I was only a temporary aberration. Then you confused me with your father, *es verdad?*'

'My...my father?' she echoed blankly.

'That sneaking, carping hypocrite, who has been chasing everything that moves in a skirt since the day you were born!' he supplied bluntly. 'That pillar of church and community, that sworn arbiter of other people's morals with the so-complacent wife. I've known about your father's affairs for years. He's well known for his...'

'Stop it!' she gasped. 'It's got nothing to do with us!'

'Has it not? Were you not hoping for the same set-up when you married me?' he contradicted roughly.

'Dear God, no!' She shuddered, shaken by the secret shame that he had forced out into the open, experiencing afresh the nudges and giggles she had endured from her classmates at school. She was equally shattered by the appalling conclusion he had drawn. 'I fell in love with you...maybe part of me did want to escape from home but——'

'Sarah *mía,*' he rhymed with burning incredulity. 'I played a leading role in the spoilt little princess's drama. I so far misunderstood the rules that I actually dared to get you pregnant. When you realised, you gave me what was undoubtedly the only honest response I ever received from you. You had hysterics and you told me that you'd never forgive me and that you didn't want my baby!'

What she read in his burnished eyes was hatred. A hatred founded on an anger that had fed on raw bitterness through the intervening years. 'You never even tried to understand how I felt,' she gasped strickenly. 'I was so scared——'

'*Sí.* Mama and Papa had not bargained on a baby. Would they consider the little princess sullied beyond repair?' he scorned.

Sarah shook her head in violent disagreement. 'I'd never even held a baby before. I was afraid I wouldn't be able to cope. I knew that a baby was usually the last straw in a shaky marriage. I was too young and I felt trapped and that was your fault!'

'Concerning the past,' Rafael breathed in blistering response, his dark eyes like hot coals on her over heated skin, 'I have nothing to say. My behaviour requires no explanation of my conscience.'

'Like hell it doesn't! Dammit, don't you dare walk away from me! You've had your say—what about me?' Trembling, she caught her unruly tongue between her teeth and watched him stride across the road to swing into his powerful car. Once she had done the walking away, the turning aside. Only in her case it had been an attempt to defuse tension and avoid an argument. And nothing, she realised now when it was too late for it to make any difference, could have been guaranteed to infuriate Rafael more. This time she was the one consumed by an angry wave of frustration and it was a new experience for her.

At home again, the twins noisily engrossed in playing in their room, Sarah paced the lounge carpet for over an hour. But it was no use... the memories wouldn't leave her alone.

At eighteen, her dreams had been of romance and irresponsibility, not of marriage and motherhood. But after one blazing confrontation with her father, Rafael had forced her to make a choice. Either she stayed on in Paris as his wife or she returned home alone. He had not even mentioned the possibility of visiting her in England. No, indeed... Rafael had known exactly how to exert the pressure. And, terrified as she had been of losing him, Sarah had agreed to that recklessly hasty marriage but her first spark of uneasy resentment and apprehension had been born that same day. All her life, her parents had employed pressure of one kind or another to make her conform. Without a second's hesitation, Rafael had utilised the same weapon.

The wedding in a foreign country, shorn of both frills and family support, had seemed curiously unreal in the aftermath and a disillusioning far cry from her youthful fantasies of the most important day of her life.

'These things are trivial,' Rafael had dismissed impatiently, surveying her with brilliant dark eyes already darkening with sensual anticipation.

On their wedding night she had been faced with the reality that Rafael was still virtually a stranger to her. In vain had she suggested that he give her a few days to adjust. His expressive mouth curling with very male amusement, he had ignored the plea, laughing when she struggled awkwardly to explain how she felt. In the bedroom, Rafael had proved to be as unashamedly dominant as he was everywhere else. She had not expected pleasure from sexual intimacy. Her upbringing had been too repressed, inescapably coloured by her mother's distaste for anything relating to the physical union between a man and a woman.

Even so, Rafael's distinct lack of inhibition had been a decided shock to her system. And nothing could have prepared her for the pain of that initiation. Had she been less miserably tense, less bitterly resentful beneath her seemingly submissive façade that night, perhaps it wouldn't have happened that way. That it had, ironically fulfilling her worst fears, had been extremely unfortunate.

'It will never be like that again,' Rafael had promised fervently, gathering her rigid body close, fighting her silent unwillingness to be held.

He had been correct but the damage had already been done. From that night on, Sarah had never been able to relax, had never been able to vocalise the raw feeling of resentment that tensed her up every time Rafael pulled her into his arms.

He had railroaded her into a relationship she wasn't ready for, refusing to allow her the smallest space in which to find her feet in a threateningly new and very demanding environment. The disillusionment of the bedroom had soon been followed by other less important but no less upsetting discoveries for Sarah. Rafael would not allow her to draw on her trust fund, disdaining what he saw as Southcott money. Sarah had not found it easy to manage on a small budget. She had been no more at ease in the kitchen, where her efforts swung between the inedible and the just passable with humiliating regularity.

Few marriages could have set sail under a heavier stress factor. Sarah had been brought up to believe that she was deeply indebted to her adoptive parents. In one fell swoop she had destroyed all their ambitious hopes for her future—her marriage to Rafael had shattered them. It had also burdened Sarah with guilt and a helpless need to try and compensate her parents for the bitter disappointment she had caused them. But in striving to please both Rafael and them she had pleased neither. And as the hostilities had hotted up rather than showing any sign of abating, Sarah had been put under intolerable pressure by the people she loved.

Not surprisingly, her self-esteem had sunk to an all-time low. She had felt horribly inadequate and Rafael's attitude towards her hadn't helped. He had taken charge of her life, taking over exactly where the Southcotts had left off, controlling her every move and treating her like a witless child in need of care and protection. At times she had wanted to scream that she was sick and tired of people telling her what to do... only she hadn't been able to let go of her frustrations that easily.

She had been taught to hide her emotions and suppress her anger. Nobody had ever told her that it was all right...indeed perfectly normal to get furiously angry with someone she loved. Nobody had ever taught her how to cope with such conflicting emotions. Rafael invariably turned discussions into fierce arguments, shooting her down in a hail of words she could not hope to match. As the months passed, Sarah's inner resentments had mounted to stifling proportions...

The bell went in three shrill, staccato bursts. It was unmistakably Karen's signature tune. Cursing under her breath, Sarah went to answer the door.

CHAPTER FOUR

KAREN erupted breathlessly through the door like a tornado. 'Rafael Alejandro is your husband and it's time you came clean!' she delivered and, as a guilty afterthought, 'Where are the kids?'

'In their room.'

'Good.' Karen took advantage of her bemusement and pressed her into the kitchen. 'Enlightenment hit me over lunch. Gilly and Ben are the picture of him!'

'I was planning to tell you,' Sarah muttered uncomfortably.

'Rubbish!' Karen shot her a glance of mingled annoyance and reproach. 'You were going to take your secrets to the grave with you!'

'Secrecy gets to be a habit.'

'I thought you'd married a waiter or a deckchair attendant or something!' Karen fumed. 'I also thought I was your best friend.'

'You are.' Squirming with guilt, Sarah sighed. 'I just don't know what you expect me to tell you...'

'What's he like in bed? No, scratch that! It was quite, quite unforgivable,' Karen retracted hurriedly as Sarah turned pale. 'Sorry. It's just one can't help wondering and putting one's foot in one's mouth by thinking out loud.'

'Don't ask me.' Sarah put the kettle on with unsteady hands. 'Take a census of public opinion.'

'Ouch,' Karen framed and ruefully released her breath. 'Enough said to be understood,' she added with unusual quietness.

Involuntarily Sarah was recalling the passion she had roused in Rafael. A look or the merest touch had been enough to communicate the primitive depth of that masculine hunger she had not then properly understood. But she had not been the only one guilty of misconceptions. Rafael had mistaken her inhibitions for shyness, her reluctance for innocence, and neither trait had displeased him. Women had been throwing themselves at Rafael since he was a teenager. One capable of coolly detaching herself from his most heated embrace to repair her lipstick had challenged the hunter in his hot-blooded temperament.

'When did you marry him?' Karen cleared her throat awkwardly. 'Or wasn't there a marriage?'

Sarah could see some justification for that question and she wasn't offended. 'We got married three weeks after we met. In Paris.'

'Three weeks?' Karen exclaimed incredulously. 'You only knew him for three weeks?'

'My father made an unscheduled visit and...he found out about Rafael,' she encapsulated with understatement, losing colour at the memory. 'It was either marry him or never see him again. We hardly knew each other. We must have been insane. I couldn't boil an egg without burning it!' She forced a laugh.

'There are more important things,' Karen said drily.

But she had failed in that field as well, she acknowledged painfully, and thumbscrews wouldn't have dragged that admission from her. Instead she managed a careless shrug. 'I was only eighteen. We had a lot of strikes against us. We had my parents doing everything they could to break us up and we didn't have much money either——'

'What?' Karen cut in. 'Elise told me that he's from a very wealthy background.'

Sarah looked at her in astonishment. 'I can't imagine where she picked up that idea.'

Karen frowned. 'Maybe I misunderstood. Sorry, I interrupted you.'

'There isn't much more. In the end, Rafael got bored. His reputation as an artist was taking off,' she murmured flatly. 'And he took off with it. End of story.'

'That was very informative, Sarah,' Karen breathed with irony. 'You spend a couple of years with a male who looks as if he could make a handshake into a whole new erotic experience and you compress him into two throwaway lines like a tax write-off! You could take the fantasy out of Disneyland.'

Sarah's lashes veiled her strained eyes. She suppressed an urge to admit that that had been more or less Rafael's opinion as well.

That night she lay awake for a long time. To be in the midst of a gathering storm and do nothing was to invite disaster. And where Rafael was concerned sitting on the fence was positively suicidal. The fence was likely to collapse while you were still sitting on it. Hours of frantic soul-searching forced her to certain conclusions, none of which eased her mental conflict.

Rafael had a legal right to see Gilly and Ben. Admitting that went against the grain but there it was, one of those facts of life that couldn't be ignored. She ought to be able to take control of the situation and act like a mature woman of twenty-five. As a rule she was calm and sensible. She could usually see both sides of an argument even when her own feelings were involved. Why should those qualities go out of the window now when she most needed her wits about her? Why had both her attempts to reason with Rafael ended in dismal failure?

And she knew why, oh, yes, she knew within her heart and her soul where only the truth could dwell. Some bonds went too deep to break. Some emotions were quite independent of pride and common sense. You didn't stop loving someone just because they hurt you. If love died so easily there would be a lot less unhappiness in the

world. In every other way her life had changed since
their separation. There was only one constant between
then and now.

It was a humiliating irony that she should grow and
mature and still retain an utterly adolescent and uncon-
trollable set of reactions to Rafael. She refused to put
a label to those feelings. After all, time had moved on
for Rafael, if not for her, and every time she saw him
she hated him just that little bit more for that reality.
Perhaps in the end that would be the saving of her, she
conceded with angry self-loathing.

She had a frantic rush to get out the next morning.
Gilly and Ben were attending a birthday barbecue after
nursery school and she not only had to search for the
present she had bought, but wrap it as well. Arriving at
work within a minute of opening time, she felt under
pressure. Summer flu had decimated the office and she
had a heap of typing to do while she greeted arriving
clients and dealt with their queries. She made elemen-
tary mistakes in letters she could normally type with her
eyes closed. By finishing time she felt like a wet rag and
that was when Rafael strolled in.

He was wearing an exquisitely tailored dove-grey suit,
cut continental fasion. The subtle sheen of the fabric
screamed expense, shaping broad shoulders and long,
lean thighs, smoothly accentuating the indolent grace of
his carriage. Aside of that disturbingly exotic quality that
was intrinsically his own, he looked like a wealthy
European businessman, polished, sophisticated and very
self-assured. A couple of typists on the way past almost
broke their necks giving his dark, virile physique a second
glance.

'Who told you where I worked?' Sarah was infuriated
by the breathless edge to her voice. She hated being taken
by surprise.

'Your neighbour was very helpful when I called at your
apartment,' Rafael imparted with a careless cool that

mocked her own heat. 'I understand that the children are otherwise occupied this afternoon, so you are free for lunch.'

Sarah's jaw dropped inelegantly. 'Lunch?'

Black-lashed golden eyes rested narrowly on her flushed face. 'Am I not suitably dressed? Why do you stare at me like this?' he demanded impatiently. 'If you have made other arrangements, unmake them.'

For two pins she would have thrown caution to the winds and lied but a native streak of sense prevented her from making that mistake. Rafael had the whip-hand. To antagonise him unnecessarily would be foolish. 'Give me a couple of minutes.'

But the submissive note stuck in her throat. She stalked into the cloakroom and took several deep, sustaining breaths. What did he want? Had he already been to see his lawyer? That would explain the suit on a male who had not even worn a tie at his own wedding. Glancing in the mirror, she grimaced. Heavens, she looked drab! Her short-sleeved white blouse and narrow green skirt looked exactly like the uniform it was. In a sudden burst of rebellion she released her hair from its tidy pleat and let the pale golden strands fan down on to her shoulders in silken disarray. She wished that she were wearing something scarlet and sleek and shocking to set Rafael back on his arrogant heels. Her forehead indented. What on earth did her appearance have to do with anything? Thoroughly irritated with herself, she raked a brush roughly through her hair.

His eyes wandered over her at a leisurely pace as she walked across the floor to join him. She reddened, furiously conscious of the odd little spur of excitement twisting in her stomach. Hopefully by the time lunch was over prolonged exposure to Rafael's chauvinistic attitudes would have taken care of that problem for her.

'How long have you been working?' he asked.

'Since I got the twins into nursery school.'

His mouth hardened. 'What do you do with them in the holidays?'

Sarah bridled. 'What do you think I do? I pay someone to look after them!'

'I think you should be at home with them,' he delivered harshly.

'Women actually got the vote this century, Rafael.'

A hard hand cupped her elbow, forcing her round to face him. 'Do you forget that I know exactly what the disadvantages of such an upbringing are? I know what it is like to be dragged up without a father, dependent on a mother who has neither the time nor the inclination to put her child's needs first!'

Enraged, Sarah flung her head back the better to stare up at the overpoweringly tall male holding her captive. 'I'm neither illiterate nor promiscuous, Rafael. It's highly unlikely that either of my children will end up stealing their next meal!'

A dark flush slowly stained his golden skin. Sarah dropped her head, shocked to the core by her own instinctive cruelty. Rafael's father had died before he was born. His mother had been a gypsy, a teenager who had found a baby an onerous burden. She had trailed him round the Spanish countryside like a piece of excess baggage, occasionally working to keep them but more often than not depending on the generosity of a series of casual lovers.

The love and security that Gilly and Ben took for granted Rafael had never had. Instead he had had to learn how to fend for himself on the streets and at the tender age of seven he had been caught stealing from a market stall. While he was in the temporary care of an orphanage, his mother, with a gypsy's fear of bureaucracy and repercussions, had taken flight. Rafael had never seen his mother again.

The authorities had traced his grandparents and handed him over to them. They in turn had passed him over to a reluctant uncle and aunt with no desire for the responsibility. Even as a child, Rafael had probably understood far too much of what was going on around him. She could picture him as a little boy with a shock of black unruly hair and bold dark eyes that challenged and just dared the world to pity him. Her throat ached, hurting her. Rafael didn't like talking about his childhood. It was his one streak of vulnerability. And once, so long ago it seemed now, she had seen that as a bond between them.

Biting back her pain, she murmured, 'I can't afford to stay at home.'

His astonishment was unhidden. 'You refused my financial support when we separated!' he reminded her angrily.

Sarah sent him a driven glance. 'At the time I didn't think you cared about me or the children. I didn't want your conscience money.'

'Conscience money?' he repeated, incensed.

'All right,' she conceded wearily. 'It probably wasn't the cleverest decision I ever made. It hasn't been easy to manage on my own but I do appreciate my independence. I live my life without interference from anybody and that's how I like it.'

He frowned down at her incredulously. 'Your parents...?'

She tilted her chin in unconscious defiance. 'If I went back to live with them, they'd keep me in the lap of luxury. But at my age I'm a little past looking to my parents for support.'

'So my children must pay the price for your false pride.' Rafael was viewing her with smouldering censure. 'If this is an example of your maturity, I am not impressed by it.'

Oh, dear heaven, give me the strength not to embark on another blazing argument, she pleaded inwardly. She had to reason with Rafael. She had to convince him that she was a good mother. But Rafael was unlikely to approve of any facet of their lifestyle. He was probably already convinced that he could offer the twins more than a small city flat and a working mother. He might even be planning to marry again. As that possibility took her by storm, she was filled with a sick, tortured fear that she did not want to examine.

A taxi dropped them at a restaurant within walking distance of her flat. 'I was not sure how much time you had,' he explained.

'I've got all afternoon.' Afraid he might translate that as some sort of fatuous hint, she muttered hurriedly, 'But I'm sure this won't take long.'

High-backed seats discreetly sectioned off the tables into little pockets of privacy. It was scarcely the setting for a detached, businesslike discussion, she thought irritably. The atmosphere was dark, intimate and candle-lit. Giving the menu a cursory glance, she picked a salad. She should have been hungry. After all, she had skipped breakfast but her appetite had vanished when Rafael appeared. Stress had scared it off. As the waiter moved away, she helped herself to a glass of wine from the bottle that had already been brought to them at Rafael's instruction.

It was a good wine. Rafael would be incapable of choosing anything less. Mellow and dry, the clear liquid bathed her tight throat in cooling silk. He had developed some very expensive tastes in the past five years, she reflected. A Lamborghini, an apartment that was the last word in location and elegance. They had to be rented, she decided. He was a rare visitor to London.

'I assume that we both intend to put the children's needs before our own personal inclinations,' Rafael drawled lazily.

It was the opening salvo of an attack but she couldn't yet figure out from which direction the attack might be coming. Still, he was much calmer and cooler than

he had been yesterday. 'That has always been my policy.'
She was pleased with her dry response.

'I want to meet them this afternoon and tomorrow I
would like to take them out somewhere.'

Alarm stole away her short-lived satisfaction. He was
not even giving her time to adjust to the prospect of his
presence in their lives. Then why should he? a saner voice
asked. Perhaps he was leaving London soon. Naturally
he would want to make immediate use of whatever time
he had left.

'Sarah...do you object to this?'

In the flickering candlelight, his golden skin was
stretched prominently over his superb bone-structure,
delineating hard angles and proud curves. He had a
Renaissance face. He could have worn silks and velvets
and gold earrings to the manner born. As the alien
thought came to fruition, she shifted uneasily on her
seat, a little like someone trying to wake up surreptitiously from a disturbing dream. She clutched her glass
tautly between her fingers, frantically questioning the
cause of her disorientation.

In his fierce, compelling gaze lay the full force of his
energy and his ruthless determination. Acute intelligence powered his direct scrutiny. A curious weakness
assailed her, her mouth running dry. 'Would there be
any point if I did?'

'None.' He lounged indolently back into the corner,
a lean hand cradling a glass with natural grace. He could
relax. He had won the first round, she acknowledged
bitterly.

'If you hurt them, I'll never forgive you,' she said
tightly.

'Why should I hurt them?'

'You can't walk into their lives and then walk back
out again when it suits you.'

He took a calm, reflective sip of wine. 'That is not
my intention.'

Sarah stiffened. 'I'm afraid I tend to judge by experience.'

An ebony brow elevated. 'You sound bitter.'

'How could I be? I got rid of you!' Sarah drained her glass, set it down with a distinct snap.

'So you were aware of what your parents did,' he said softly, dangerously softly.

'No, I wasn't!' she contradicted vehemently. 'I was here and you were in New York. My mother was ill and I was worried sick about her...'

Rafael made a scathing sound of dismissal. 'There was nothing wrong with your mother. Her sudden illness was merely another ploy.'

'Yes,' Sarah allowed heavily. 'But I didn't know that then. My fears for her health were very real. And what did you do? You——'

'I attempted to break the deadlock,' he interrupted her again with greater heat.

'Was that what you called it? You gave me forty-eight hours to join you in New York. I said no and that was that. I never saw you again. Sometimes I wondered if I'd dreamt you up. Only dreams tend to be kinder than reality!'

'I came back to England. Where were you?'

Sarah had become suddenly taut and when a waiter refilled her glass she clasped it gratefully. Holding something made it easier for her to keep her hands steady.

'The only communication I received from you was through a lawyer,' he continued with caustic bite. 'A demand for a divorce. So much faith as you had in me, *gatita!*'

'My father put detectives on you while you were in New York.'

'I know that!' he cut in rawly. 'And five years ago I might have explained myself to you but not now.'

A hollow laugh escaped her. 'An explanation would have seriously taxed your ingenuity, Rafael. When a woman spends the night in your hotel room there isn't much leeway for error...'

'It might have been innocent.'

Sarah gulped down another fortifying mouthful of wine. 'With you in the starring role? Are you kidding?' she demanded with a reasonable pretence of mocking amusement, but in spite of her determination to remain cool the old anger was spiralling up from the tight coil of tension inside her. 'I wasn't surprised. I can be honest about that now. I never trusted you. I was always waiting for it to happen. By that stage, I was sure it already had...'

Rafael was watching her with unnerving concentration.

'You have the morals of an alleycat.' That last sentence fled her lips before she could seal them and tremulously turn her head away, fighting hard to recover her self-control.

'Yet you said nothing of these suspicions at the time.' Long fingers deftly coiled round the bottle and tilted it over her half-empty glass. 'I did not realise how you felt,' he positively purred.

'You were too b...blasted insensitive!' As his mouth quirked, she flushed with embarrassment.

'It seems I must have been,' he murmured soothingly. 'Have some more wine. The vintage appears to agree with your palate.'

'I'm not hungry,' she muttered in partial apology as she pushed her plate away and picked up her glass again.

A splintering tension she didn't understand suddenly held her still beneath the glittering onslaught of his golden gaze. 'No woman was ever more loved than you were.'

'You married me to get me into bed,' she muttered bluntly. 'Why wrap it up?'

'Sarah.' A sunbrowned forefinger idly circled over the back of her clenched hand and hot shivers ran through her, setting up a chain reaction of responses that shook her rigid. Under her blouse, her breasts peaked into painful tightness. Her nerve-endings all seemed to be centred at screaming point beneath his finger. Aghast by the sensations, she couldn't move.

'If I had insisted you would have shared my bed before I married you,' he asserted with lazy arrogance. 'You know that, I know that. That is not why I married you.'

She curved back defensively into her seat, edgily removing her fingers from reach of his careless caress. But she could still feel the imprint of his flesh, heating her blood and murdering her ability to think straight. Her heartbeat had accelerated to an insane tempo and it wasn't steadying even yet. What on earth was the matter with her?

Rafael withdrew his hand with a sudden brilliant, blazing smile that made it difficult for her to breathe. 'We will talk about that later,' he dismissed, resting his ebony head back, narrowed tawny eyes gleaming with rich satisfaction. 'Where were you when I returned to England?'

The direct question, thrown without warning made her freeze. Gooseflesh prickled on the exposed parts of her body. She evaded his gaze. 'I was in a clinic. That was true,' she shared jerkily. 'The doctor said I would miscarry if I didn't have complete peace and quiet. I was there for weeks and it was incredibly boring——'

'You were ill?' Rafael had lost colour, abandoned relaxation. *'Dios!'* he ground out viciously. 'If I had your father here now, I would——'

'You didn't try very hard to find me,' she said helplessly.

'I had no desire to find you when I believed you had had an abortion,' he proffered fiercely. 'Your father made it clear that it was too late.'

'You didn't have much faith in me.'

'Their hold on you was greater than mine.'

'No, it wasn't,' she corrected unsteadily. 'I was being torn apart. You hated them and they hated you and I was out in no man's land, trying to keep the peace. Sometimes I just wanted to run away and leave you all to it.'

His expressive eyes had chilled. 'I have never forgotten how I was insulted by your family.'

'Yet you had so much in common with them,' Sarah dared.

'Qué te pasa?' Rafael grated incredulously. 'What's the matter with you?'

Her smile was awry. 'To both of you I was an object, a possession. They bought me with adoption, you bought me with marriage. Let's face it, it was an ownership dispute. They wouldn't let go and you wouldn't share me. It was a tug of war and inevitably the rope had to break.'

'Perhaps it amuses you to be facetious.'

'I don't find it amusing even now,' Sarah confessed. 'In a sense you were even more selfish than they were. Possession is nine-tenths of the law. I don't think I can have come under the context of fixtures and fittings when you took me away from them. You didn't steal me, did you? You had legal title.'

'Sarah.' It was a warning growl, given between gritted teeth.

Her head was feeling oddly light but she was enjoying herself. 'Didn't you ever wonder why I was the very centre of their world? Or didn't you care? They don't like each other very much. They don't talk because they've nothing to talk about unless I'm there or I'm provoking some sort of crisis. They should have split up years ago but they stayed together because they were offered a child. And unfortunately that child was me...'

'You are not responsible for their marital problems.' Rafael was patently uninterested in the subject.

Her soft mouth curved down. 'Of course you probably gathered all that from the beginning. I was too close to see it. I thought the way they were was somehow all my fault. In their own twisted, self-centred fashion they care about me. It was very, very hard for them to accept that I was never going to live with them again.'

Black luxuriant lashes partially veiled his keen scrutiny. 'When did that miracle occur?'

'My great-aunt offered me a home just before the twins were born. Up until last year I was living with her in Truro.'

'Truro?' he echoed.

'It's in Cornwall.'

'I know where this place is!' he grated. 'Are you saying that you have been there ever since our separation? I believed you were living under the protection of your parents.'

'When did you last fight off a dragon and rescue a fair maiden, Rafael?' she enquired gently.

His jawline clenched. 'Explain this talk of dragons.'

Sarah fingered a prawn off her plate and nibbled at it abstractedly. The tip of her tongue darted out to lick her lips clean. Glancing up, she found tiger's eyes intent on her soft, full mouth. 'Only helpless little creatures with fluff between their ears need protection now the dragons have gone. I've never had much taste for iron bars and bossy people. Yet I married you.' Slowly she shook her head over that riddle. 'That's called leaping out of the frying-pan straight into the fire.'

'What did you do in Truro?' Rafael probed darkly.

'I did whatever I wanted to do,' she said truthfully. 'Letitia was the only unconventional member of my mother's family. Before I met her, I had lived twenty years on this planet without realising that freedom is every individual's inalienable right. Freedom from other people's wishes, expectations and demands. You have no idea how glorious it was just to be myself after I got over the guilt. Yes, it took me a while to work up the courage to spread my wings but in the end I was putting in more flying time than an airline stewardess.'

Tempted by another prawn, Sarah reached for it. 'These are really good.' She paused. 'Why are you looking at me like that?'

His nostrils flared. 'What did doing whatever you want entail?'

Sarah munched unselfconsciously at her prawn and thought for a second or two. 'I really don't think that's any of your business any more.'

'It is very much my business while you remain my wife.'

'You sound like Gordon...well, the way Gordon would like to be if he had the guts—but his wife was a feminist. He's secretly terrified of feminists.'

Sunbrowned fingers were beating out a soundless tattoo on the edge of the table. Rafael's body language was so gloriously, exquisitely self-expressive, Sarah reflected with satisfaction. For once she had managed to turn the tables. Later she would feel pain, that went without saying, but for now a patina of breezy insouciance was more of a cushion to her decimated pride than the role of embittered and soon to be ex-wife. 'What about that long, tall blonde you're living with? Are you thinking of marrying her?'

The fingers tensed, stretched and stilled. 'I am married to you.'

Sarah produced a laugh that should have qualified for a champagne tribute. 'Since when has that inhibited you? Then as you once told me,' she said playfully, 'sex is not a serious business.'

Blazing golden eyes crashed a collision course with hers. Her heartbeat gave a sick thud. 'Suzanne——'

'Oh, is that her name? Rather elegant...it suits her.' With a generously bright smile, Sarah took masochism to new and serious limits. She relocated her glass as if it were an anchor. 'Does she cook? If she cooks as well, you've got it made, Rafael. Speaking for myself, however, if I should ever remarry it will be to someone—to borrow a phrase from Karen—who is seriously rich and who wouldn't dream of expecting me to soil my little princess hands in anything so mundane as a kitchen. You said once that I was born to be a rich man's toy. Of course you were pretty close to starvation at the time but you really ought to have added, in the interests of fairness, that cosseted little toys have a wonderful time in the rich man's playroom because that's where they belong.'

Colour lay in a definitive arc over his angular cheekbones. Undertones and tension and seething emotion were heating the atmosphere to boiling point. Sarah revelled in the awareness. It was like a stimulating drug racing through her bloodstream. She could not recall when she had last enjoyed herself so much.

'Suzanne——' he gritted.

Sarah held up a hand. 'One little hint. Toss an unplucked chicken at her and ask her to whip up something exotic for six unexpected guests. That's the sort of high-jump that picks out the women from the girls. I should know.'

'Suzanne is married to one of my best friends.'

Sarah opened her eyes wide. 'And she runs round your apartment in a little tiny bathrobe, offering you breakfast after she gets out of your shower? It must be a very open marriage. Rather like ours, I expect,' she tacked on. 'Don't you think it's marvellous that we can sit here being perfectly civilised after all these years?'

'I think it is obscene!' he raked at her. 'We did not have that sort of relationship.'

'No, it was rather one-sided in that direction, wasn't it? You strayed and I stayed home.'

He was breathing shallowly. 'I also think you are trying to shock me.'

'Do you think I could?' Sarah was almost mesmerised by the savage brilliance of his stare and the surprising fact that Rafael was swallowing what she said without exploding. 'What would it take?'

He flicked her a glance of flaring, cutting perception. 'Considerably more than a very clumsy attempt to make me jealous.'

Sarah didn't think about what she did next. She acted on instinct. She plunged upright and sent the contents of her glass flying at him. As soon as it was done, she was appalled by her own behaviour.

'Sit down!' Rafael roared at her, snatching up a pristine napkin. 'I don't think lunch was such a good idea.' Sarah fled, her courage spent.

She emerged from the restaurant into a heavy downpour. Rain was falling in sheets, bouncing back off the dusty pavements again. Within a minute Sarah was drenched, her thin blouse plastered to her skin, her skirt clinging damply to her thighs. She was in an emotional daze, devastated by the surge of incredible anger that had driven her into an act that was quite out of character. Dimly it occurred to her that she had done quite a few things that were out of character in recent days.

She went haywire in Rafael's vicinity. A couple of glasses of wine on an empty stomach and she was suddenly treating him to a floorshow! He had invited her to lunch solely to discuss Gilly and Ben and what had he got? Well, he certainly hadn't got the chilly little civilised chat he had undoubtedly expected. I am married to you, he had said without even a human twinge of discomfiture. And she had wanted to kill him . . . slowly and with many refined tortures and not an ounce of mercy.

Saving face had been uppermost in her mind. Or so she had believed. It had suddenly become overwhelmingly important that Rafael should believe that his departure from her life had been a blessing in disguise.

Only Rafael had somehow understood her better than she understood herself. Clumsy. The word was like a poison dart digging deep into her oversensitive skin. As an attractive woman, Sarah had little confidence in her powers to attract. That really hadn't bothered her until her particular *bête noire* sauntered back on to her horizon again, exploding her calm, demolishing her wits and flinging her into violent turmoil all over again. She had gone right over the top inside that restaurant and he had let her talk herself into the grave. And not for the first time, she conceded unhappily, drawn unwillingly back into the past.

Eighteen months into their marriage, she had been simmering like a pressure-cooker on too high a heat. She had taken a good hard look at herself and she hadn't liked what she saw. She had had no identity beyond that of Rafael's wife and the Southcotts' daughter. The real Sarah couldn't defend herself because she simply didn't know who she was. She spent her time constantly striving to measure up to other people's expectations and apologising for her apparent failings. In short she was a doormat, who lacked the aggression to demand the freedom to be herself.

She had challenged Rafael's dominance on one score alone. He had wanted her to have a baby. She had carefully avoided even discussing the idea, changing the subject whenever it was raised.

It was a minor incident which ironically had triggered the tension that had been building between her and Rafael for months. One of his models repeatedly wandering half naked round the apartment had set Sarah's temper off. In the grip of suppressed fury over the fashion in which the model had simply ignored her strictures, Sarah had informed Rafael that she didn't want the woman in her home ever again. Rafael had called that unreasonable. Sarah had responded very unreasonably by emptying a drawer into a suitcase and threatening to leave.

'You're not going back to them,' Rafael had assured her with raw, blistering emphasis.

'This has nothing to do with my parents,' she had whispered in sudden despair. 'This has to do with me for a change. Me...my feelings...nobody else!'

But he hadn't understood; he hadn't recognised that she was at the end of her tether and the storm in a teacup had blown up into a hurricane. That night, Rafael had disposed of her birth control pills and had made love to her coolly, deliberately and with none of the tenderness that he usually employed.

Six weeks later, she had learnt that she was pregnant. In the scene which followed both of them had said some pretty unforgivable things. Afterwards Sarah had promised herself that she would never again allow Rafael to enforce his wishes over her own. A constraint had leapt up between them long before her father had phoned to tell her that her mother was ill.

She had been packing when Rafael emerged from his studio.

'What are you doing?'

She straightened reluctantly from her task. 'Mother's not well. I'm booked on an evening flight.'

Brilliant dark eyes raked her with glinting incredulity. 'And this is the first I am to know of your plans?'

She turned pale under threat of an argument.

Rafael sank with deceptive indolence down on to the deep sill of the window behind him. 'What is the matter with her?'

Sarah made a grudging explanation, on defensive alert for the first sign of contempt. 'It could be her heart,' she completed anxiously.

'It could be her imagination.'

'That's a despicable thing to say.'

'My exhibition opens in New York in ten days,' he reminded her grimly. 'We have to be there in——'

'I know.'

'I want you with me.' His jawline squared. 'I don't want you to go to England now. Your father has been premature. When your mother has had results of these tests——'

'No,' she broke in stiffly. 'I'm going now.'

Dark colour barred his high cheekbones. 'I don't want you to go. That should mean something to you,' he said softly.

It was the familiar crack of a whip over her head, telling her exactly what her limitations were. Silently she began folding another garment as if she hadn't heard him. It was her only defence.

'Sarah…we should not be apart now. You are carrying my child. It is selfish of your father to distress you like this,' he protested angrily. 'But if you must go I will accompany you.'

In spite of her protests, he had, and of course there had been no relaxation for her in the days which followed. Rafael and her parents under one roof would have driven any peacekeeper's nerves to screaming point.

'She's pretending,' Rafael had diagnosed her mother's health bluntly within hours. 'You can travel to New York with me.'

Outraged on her mother's behalf, Sarah had righteously refused and reproached him for his insensitivity, but she had planned to join him within the week. When it came time for her to leave, however, Louise Southcott had suffered a relapse. Another week had drifted by before Rafael presented her with an ultimatum.

On the phone he cut ruthlessly through her efforts to make safe conversation. 'Your parents are destroying our marriage,' he interrupted. 'I think you have a decision to make. Them or me. I won't wait forever. I am not a pet dog, *querida*.'

'You're not——'

'The fool you take me for? I have run out of patience,' he bit out, anger transforming his husky voice into a throaty growl. 'You have forty-eight hours. If you're not with me before the deadline I'll assume that you've decided to stay with Mama and Papa forever. But should you decide to honour your marital vows, *muñeca mia,* you have made your last visit to your parents' home.'

'You can't threaten me like that,' she gasped.

'The threat is a promise, *querida.* You must choose between us. I will no longer stand for their interference in our lives. I have stood enough. Your place as my wife is with me, not with them,' he delivered harshly. 'If you cannot acknowledge that reality, I cannot continue to think of you as my wife.'

'You can't give me a choice like that . . .'

'Can't I? I believe I just have. And I should have done it sooner.'

He had asked the impossible of her at a time when she had genuinely believed that her mother was developing a heart condition. Her pride, too often battered by his dominance, had warmed to the knowledge that she would for once stand firm. Even so, it was with a fast-beating heart that she had let that deadline approach, acquainted as she was with the volatility of Rafael's temperament . . .

As the rain slackened off, she came back to the present with a jolt.

CHAPTER FIVE

'CRISTO, Sarah!' A powerful hand fastened on her shoulder and spun her round. 'You are soaked through.'

She tried to shake free of his grasp. 'Leave me alone!'

'No!' It was raw and unequivocal. Shrugging off his jacket, he draped it round her. His body heat and an evocatively masculine scent that she had almost forgotten enclosed her chilled skin and yet still she shivered.

Her flat was just round the corner. She walked fast, not looking at him. Inside the lift the atmosphere was suffocatingly tense. With a flourish she removed his jacket but before she could return it he closed the distance between them. He slid long fingers very slowly into the damp tangle of her hair. Fierce dark eyes searched her pale, upturned face. Heat rushed up to the surface of her fair skin.

'Por dios, Sarah,' he breathed raggedly. 'What is it that you want from me?'

A dull ache stirred in the pit of her stomach. The thump of her heartbeat filled her eardrums. An overpowering sexual excitement unlike anything she had ever experienced had her entrapped, preventing her from moving away. Yet she didn't want to move away. That part of her that incredulously and finally recognised what she was feeling was instinctively greedy for the breathtaking high of awareness to continue. It brought her alive. It was heady, new and terrifying.

A brown forefinger brushed the base of her throat where a tiny pulse was going crazy. His hand was not quite steady. She stopped breathing. Rafael was not breathing either. He was watching her with burning intensity. His other hand skated down to the shallow indentation of her spine, pulling her into the hard cradle of his pelvis. She knew she only had to say a word and he would free her but she couldn't find that word, didn't want to speak it. She knew that just as *he* knew it, her secret no longer a secret, his knowledge thrown back at her by the glittering onslaught of his narrowed stare. He lowered his dark head so gradually that she trembled before he engulfed her mouth in the scorching heat of his.

Shock reverberated through her but shock was swiftly drowned by sensation. Her hands clenched convulsively into his broad shoulders. His tongue penetrated hotly between her lips, imitating another far more elemental possession, and the ground rocked and fell away beneath her feet. It was a savage awakening to a hunger that had no boundaries, a hunger that boldly seized and controlled.

She was weak and dizzy, wildly disorientated, when he released her mouth and vented a stifled groan into her hair. 'I don't know you like this,' he muttered roughly, angrily.

If he had freed her immediately she would have fallen. Her legs didn't feel as though they belonged to her any more. She was afraid to test her voice. Her body felt alien, unfamiliar. Taking a jerky step back from him, she bent her head over her bag to fumble for her key. So that's what it is like, so that is what I was supposed to feel, she was thinking in a fever of disbelief.

'I suggest that we vacate the lift,' Rafael murmured gently.

A minute later he reached over her shoulder and extracted the key from her shaking fingers to unlock the door. Her arm brushed against his hard, flat stomach and she flinched away from the contact, suddenly gripped by a very basic need to put as much space as possible between them.

'When do you collect the children?'

'I don't. A girl on the ground floor is giving them a lift back. Her daughter's at the same school and she's helping at the party,' Sarah volunteered in a strained rush, taking refuge in unnecessary detail. 'Now, if you'll excuse me, I'll get changed.'

As she turned towards her bedroom door, a strong hand enclosed hers and tugged her relentlessly back. 'But why should I excuse you when I can help you?' Rafael enquired in a silky soft purr.

Her lashes fluttered in bemusement. He couldn't possibly mean what she had thought he had meant for a crazy moment. 'H...help me?'

'Why not?' A sunbrowned fingertip traced the tremulous curve of her swollen mouth, skimmed with aching slowness along her delicate jawbone and finally came to rest in a tiny, blue-veined hollow at the base of her slender throat. By the time he reached that point, every skin-cell in her body was behaving as though it had a life and a purpose all of its own.

Clashing unwarily with luminescent gold challenge, she could feel her hold on reality loosening even more. 'Don't...' she whispered shakily.

'You speak with such conviction,' he mocked.

Alarm bells rang loudly in her head as his measuring gaze dropped to the prominent thrust of her small, high breasts and lingered on the pointed buds pushing against the damp cotton, damning indictments of her response to him. He was very still, dull coins of colour overlying his hard cheekbones, his breathing shallow and audible.

'You say "don't",' he noted in a low-pitched growl.

A peculiar lassitude was sweeping over her. Time seemed to have slowed down to a third of its normal speed.

'But I say *sí*...I say yes,' he completed.

In dumb shock she watched brown fingers drop to the first button on her blouse and expertly slide it free. For an endless moment he paused and the silence became a thunderbeat of unbearable tension before he deftly moved on to the next. She was paralysed, unable to think, unable to move, unable to protest. What was happening between them was unreal. An apparently careless forefinger unhooked the front clasp of her bra. The silk dropped away and he curved a dark hand in a possessive statement over one pouting breast. Sarah shivered violently, shutting her eyes as though by denying sight she might deny all responsibility.

With his other hand he pressed her into the invasive heat of his thighs. 'Feel what you are doing to me,' he invited hoarsely.

She could not have been unaware. Against her stomach she could feel the mounting male power of him, the predatory readiness of every leashed line of his abrasively masculine body. A drowning, debilitating weakness quivered through her lower limbs. That strange and increasingly painful ache kicked hard at her stomach again. Involuntarily she leant into him for support.

His thumb grazed a swollen nipple and she gasped, her bones melting and coalescing beneath her skin. Holding her upright, he bent his dark head and seized the taut crest between his teeth before laving the sensitive flesh with a tormenting tongue tip. Her fingers dug fiercely into his arm, a cry forced from deep in her throat as shudders of delight ripped and tore through her body.

He said something raw in his own language and his hand pushed up her skirt, dealing summarily with the hindrance, smoothing over the trembling silken length of her thigh. A jolt of electric anticipation stabbed at her, leaving her limp and pliant as a rag doll in his arms. Her flesh ached for him and she was devastated by that discovery. It rewrote and overturned everything she knew about herself. One last shred of sanity remained to her and it could only tell her, this can't be real, this isn't really happening. She was caught up in emotions and sensations quite beyond her control.

'Rafael...this...no,' she hardly knew what she was saying, never mind what she had intended to say.

'No?' Her skirt parted company with her hipbones and pooled round her feet. A determined hand splayed across her hips, crushing her against him. Smouldering tiger's eyes currented into her dazed vision, flaming a purely sexual intent. 'No is not a word I am inclined to listen to in the state that I am in.'

He swept her up in his arms and kicked the bedroom door wide. He tumbled her down on the bed, following her there in an almost instantaneous motion. Impatient hands disposed of the remainder of her clothing. He was indifferent to the sound of ripping lace but she welcomed the rapacious savagery of his demanding mouth. His mouth, oh, God, his mouth. The hot, hard angularity of his body on hers was an unbelievable pleasure and the burning urgency of his hands made her cry out, defenceless against the wild, explosive agony of need that he had induced.

'Please...please,' she gasped, driven to a torturous peak of excitement.

He parted her thighs with hands that were almost violent and thrust into her powerfully, suddenly. She felt pain but pain was nothing to the raw, incredible intensity of the pleasure. She shattered into a million tiny pieces and then she was falling...falling...falling with an astounded sense of wondering discovery and the most glorious feeling of utter, endless peace. As Rafael shuddered in the tight circle of her arms, she was assailed by a wholly intoxicating delight in her own femininity.

The strong muscles of his back contracted beneath her covetous fingers. So that is what it is like, she thought dazedly, idly running an uncontrollably possessive hand over golden skin that had the sensuous appeal of oiled silk to her worshipping touch. But far from sharing her own relaxation, Rafael's lithe magnificent length was as whipcord tense as a coiled spring. In the silence a shard of fear pierced her but she blindly fought it off. She did not want to think further than five minutes into the future. Anything more would be threatening. Anything more would detract from the tremendous sense of achievement she was experiencing. Rafael still wanted her. Magically and quite miraculously, Rafael still wanted her.

'You're very quiet,' she whispered uneasily.

'You expect conversation as well?' He lifted his dark, tousled head and released her from his weight, rolling over in the tangle of sheets without looking at her. 'You have just fulfilled my every fantasy. Conversation seems a little superfluous.'

She paled. 'That sounds like sarcasm.'

'Such acute perception. Where do you plan for us to go from here?' he gritted roughly.

Was he afraid that she was trying to trap him back into their marriage? Humiliated by the suspicion, she muttered in an impulsive rush, 'This doesn't have to mean anything.' She hesitated. 'I mean . . . I don't expect anything from you. If you like you can just walk out that door and we can forget this ever happened . . .'

He reared up, brilliant eyes flashing in stunned collision with hers. His hand anchored into the hair streaming across the pillow. 'I think you forget who you are speaking to.'

So he didn't want that escape route. An inner glow warmed her. 'The traffic through my bedroom really isn't that heavy,' she murmured with a hectic flush on her cheeks.

His fingers twisted painfully amongst the pale, golden strands of her hair but Sarah didn't object. She was fascinated by the play of strong emotion on his dark, golden features. For a second he had looked savagely angry, yet what could he possibly have to be angry about? She had not initiated that shameless seduction scene in the hall. Rafael had made all the moves and Rafael, in spite of appearances, never acted on impulse. The arts of calculation came as naturally to him as breathing. He was the most shockingly manipulative male she had ever come across. That overpoweringly masculine ego of his ought to be glorying in the fact that he had at last received the response he had always wanted from her.

Somewhere in the still-scrambled depths of her brain she realised that she hadn't a clue what she was doing and there was something insidiously reassuring about the admission. It excused her from responsible behaviour, freed her from the conventional fetters that made life so very uneventful even if they also made it safe. Be a little reckless now and again, Letitia had once urged her impatiently. Still headily in the hold of newly learnt sensuality, Sarah could not prevent her fingertips from wandering over his muscular chest, snarling into whorls of crisp, curling black hair. Reckless, she tasted dizzily, quite unaware of his unresponsive stillness as her heavy eyes slid shut, reckless felt good...indeed reckless felt like a passport to heaven.

When she woke up, she was totally disorientated. It was still daylight. A dazed look crossed her sleepy face. Slowly she sat up, wincing at unfamiliar aches and pains. She had a headache and a raging thirst as well. Memory came back like a poison arrow thudding into a target. A wave of scorching heat enveloped her body and then drained gradually away, leaving her shivering in horrified aftershock.

Oh, dear God, what had she done...what had she done? she asked herself in anguish. How could she have let this happen? How could a simple lunch-date have turned into a disaster of such appalling proportions?

But she knew. Oh, yes, she knew. Where Rafael was involved, nothing was ever simple and nothing was ever quite as it seemed. Had he been amused by the revelation that the frigid wife he had left behind now trembled and threatened to burst into flame if he so much as skated a provocative fingertip over the back of her hand? Her stomach constricted in sick distress.

In defiance of her own wretched vulnerability she had been determined to show him that she had long since come to terms with the break-up of their marriage. Reflecting on the means she had used to demonstrate that point, Sarah cringed. Her bitterness and her jealousy had goaded her into excess and, as if that had not been enough, she had proved to be as naïve about her own sexuality as an adolescent. Rafael had understood exactly what was happening to her in that restaurant and Rafael, in time-honoured tradition, had homed in on her weakest point of defence. Well, at least there was nothing new in that. In a fight, Rafael was like a warrior in mortal combat. There were no holds barred, no allowances made for a less able partner.

She had never had a strong head for alcohol yet he had topped up her glass and lounged back indolently while she chattered her way into World War III. He must have known that she was in no fit state to know what she was doing. But, unbelievable as it seemed to her, Rafael had set out quite deliberately to seduce her. And her subconscious mind, for so long disciplined into subjection, had had the last laugh after all... hadn't it?

With fingers that were all thumbs, she pulled on her robe. Someone like Karen fell in love at least four times a year. Karen skated on the sparkly tinsel surface of romance and deftly avoided collisions. But in a Paris street, Sarah had met crash... bang... wallop with the equivalent of a major pile-up and ever since she had lived in the accident zone.

Five years ago, she had put her feelings for Rafael into a compartment. She had locked the door and thrown away the key. She would have burnt at the stake sooner than admit to anyone how she still felt about Rafael. It wasn't socially acceptable to continue to want a man who had kicked you in the teeth. By the same yardstick, such self-knowledge was a constant source of self-loathing. She was as much in love with Rafael as she had ever been and undoubtedly a psychologist would tell her that she was a masochist. After all, she conceded with a surge of sudden bitterness, Rafael didn't know the half of what he had done to her.

The final cost of repeatedly defying her father had been terrifying. In remembrance, she shuddered, struggling to close out all recollection of the nightmare months when the most basic of human rights had been wrested from her. The loss of her freedom and the terror that she would never regain it had somewhat diluted the effect of Rafael's infidelity. Survival came before pride. Sarah had learnt that lesson within weeks. Locked away in that clinic and deprived of all contact with the outside world, she had swiftly realised that Rafael was her only possible ally against her father. Only Rafael hadn't come to slay her dragons for her. Surrendering that last hope of rescue had been like losing the will to live for a time and the memories of how she had felt could still wake her up in a cold sweat of fear in the middle of the night.

Learning now that Rafael had not deliberately abandoned her had cut through the protective layer of her bitter antagonism and distrust. And this...this, she registered, surveying the disordered bed with a sinking sensation in the pit of her stomach, this was the catastrophic result of letting her guard down in Rafael's radius. Shame was eating her alive. Thank God he had had the decency to leave. Clumsily pulling open the bedroom door, she walked into the lounge and froze on the threshold.

Three pairs of identical dark eyes turned to her. Gilly and Ben were sitting crosslegged at Rafael's feet.

'I...I didn't know you were home yet,' she stammered.

'We've been home for ages,' Ben volunteered cheerfully. 'We had to be quiet 'cos you were sleeping.'

'You should have woken me up.' Fiddling nervously with the sash of her robe, Sarah avoided Rafael's piercing scrutiny, afraid of what she might see there. Amusement, triumph or contempt—it didn't really matter. Nothing could wipe out her agonised awareness that just a couple of hours ago she had been sobbing with satisfaction in his arms.

'We were busy,' Gilly told her. 'Daddy was telling us a story.'

'Daddy?' Sarah interrupted, ludicrously unprepared for the ease with which that designation tripped off her daughter's tongue.

Ben gave her a miniature male-to-dumb-female look of reproach. 'How could you move house and not 'member to say where the new house was? Daddy didn't know where to find us.'

Gilly nodded sagely. 'We got lost and now Daddy's found us we're going to be a family.'

Sarah's teeth ground together. 'We're a family now.'

'But we look like Daddy. We don't look like you,' Ben objected, sending pain shooting through his mother as he studied Rafael with unhidden admiration. 'Or like Grandad or Grandma.'

'And we're Span-nish 'cos Daddy's Span-nish,' Gilly sounded out importantly. 'Spanish people live in Spain and talk Spanish.'

'Ethnic origins seem to have figured heavily on the agenda,' Sarah breathed tightly.

As Gilly broke back into excitable speech, Rafael moved a silencing hand. 'I want both of you to play in your room while I talk to your mother.'

Under Sarah's arrested gaze, the twins scrambled up and did as they were told. True, their feet dragged on the way out but they didn't argue. Rafael jerked invisible strings and her children leapt to do his bidding. They could not have been home much more than an hour and he had already won their respect and their acceptance.

He had achieved that without her help or even her presence. Then did not like identify with like? Mutual recognition had clearly been matched by mutual appreciation.

Rafael rose fluidly upright and suddenly the room seemed small and airless. Fully dressed, he put her at a further disadvantage. Dark eyes, impenetrable as night, rested on her. Her anger mysteriously ebbed away to be replaced by a desperate uncertainty.

'I thought you'd already gone.' She was determined to mask the jumble of hopelessly confused emotions that had taken hold of her without warning.

An eloquent black brow lifted. 'Even as a teenager, I had more finesse.'

Painful red stained her complexion and she turned away in an uncoordinated half-circle. 'You said something about wanting to see the children tomorrow.' Her fingernails scored purple crescents in her clenched palms. 'You can see them whenever you like. I'm prepared to be reasonable.'

'Avoiding the issue is an art form with you, *gatita*.' Tiny hairs prickled at the nape of her neck. 'Is this all you have to say to me?'

He had the most gorgeous, growling accent. Momentarily she was unsure whether it was nerves or an overt and crucifying awareness of him that was responsible for her inability to concentrate. 'I intend to forget what happened.' Her voice was shamefully unsteady.

'This is very trite. From any woman but you, it would be almost unbelievable.' His roughened intonation alerted her to the darkness of his mood. 'You wanted me, Sarah——'

'When I was falling down drunk!' she cut in, angrily repudiating the charge as she moved restively over to the window and crossed her arms over her breasts. She ached to be held by him. She could feel it inside her; a spreading weakness and terrible vulnerability that she had to find the strength to deny. She had given herself with a naïve sense of joy and wonder. She could not bear to have reality destroy the last remnants of the dream.

'You were not drunk. You were not even close to that state.' With characteristic candour and no small amount of derision, Rafael ruthlessly demolished the excuse. 'You wanted me and I gave you what you wanted. Do you know why?'

She laced her arms even tighter. 'I don't want to know.'

'I was curious,' he confided cruelly. 'Insatiably curious.'

Sarah recoiled. Brilliant dark eyes lingered assessingly on her growing pallor. 'As an experiment, *gatita,* it was remarkably informative. Five years ago, you were ice in my bed. And now? Now you throw yourself at me with positive enthusiasm!'

A shudder of acute mortification snaked through her taut limbs. 'That's a lie!'

'Is it? Then I do not presume to flatter myself with the belief that my experience with you was unique.' The rawness of each accented syllable suggested gritted teeth. She looked at him properly for the first time since she had entered the room. Anger barely contained irradiated his strong, dark features, lightening his golden skin. His jawline was savagely taut. Rafael was making a very high-profile attempt to restrain his hot temper.

Sarah blinked rapidly, more awake to his anger than his meaning. 'I don't understand.'

'Don't you?' he breathed, and she could feel sparks ready to ignite in the suffocating atmosphere. 'I am not the only man you have invited to your bed in recent years. This...this was obvious...so obvious that it was an insult!'

'An insult?' she parroted, foolishly rooted to the spot.

'You could not wait to demonstrate your lack of inhibition. You wanted me to know that you had had other lovers!'

The floor seemed to be heaving under her feet. Rafael invariably saw wheels within wheels, hidden things in dark corners and complexity and double meaning where none existed. He had a naturally suspicious nature. Briefly she didn't know whether to be amused or offended by his assumption. She ought to be laughing, she decided numbly. She couldn't understand why she wasn't laughing because really it was hysterically funny. Only a suicidal maniac would have reeled away from their marriage to go off in pursuit of another man.

'We are still m...married.' She stumbled clumsily over the reminder. 'And there haven't been any other——'

'You were quick to disabuse me of that notion earlier,' he rebutted contemptuously. 'What we shared was a casual sexual encounter and that reflects glory upon neither one of us.'

Sarah was shaking. She dug her fingers into the back of a high-backed chair, afraid that if she let go she might fall. Casual? *Casual?* Rafael had practically torn her clothes off. Phrases like indecent haste and a violent lack of control seemed more apt. But then what did she know about such things? She had no basis for comparison. Certainly Rafael had never behaved like that during their marriage. Then he had been very cool, very controlled...except once, her memory adjusted and her skin heated as she recalled the night that the twins had been conceived without her agreement. After that, he had never touched her again. Casual, she tasted again, retreating from the past and cringing from the present. Every moral principle she possessed revolted against the knowledge that Rafael had taken her out of some sort of cruel and lustful impulse.

'You bastard.' Abusing him hurt her throat but then she did not believe that there was a single part of her that wasn't hurting.

A scathing brow lifted. 'Almost,' he breathed disconcertingly. 'But not quite. And no doubt you are ready to accuse me of the double standard, *es verdad?* I am not ashamed of that. You are the mother of my children.'

Rafael was a throwback to the caves and he was not about to apologise for the fact. Anger was coming slowly but surely to Sarah's rescue, raising her from what felt like the very depths of humiliation. Evidently Rafael had expected her to exist in suspended animation since his desertion. After all, if she did not want him how could she possibly be attracted by any other man?

Women fell in the aisles round Rafael. He wasn't conceited but he could not have been unaware of his own worth. His 'love them and leave them' reputation with her sex ran little short of notoriety. He was fantastic copy for gasping female gossip columnists. And this was the male standing here in her lounge, unashamedly outraged by the suspicion that his estranged wife might have dared to find solace in another man's arms? Where the blazes did he get the brazen nerve from? How dared he?

Golden eyes splintered into her in a near-physical assault. 'And the traffic through your bedroom will be considerably lighter in the future.'

Sarah's sole desire now was to retaliate in kind. Temper lanced through her in a wild thrust of aggression. 'I'd love to know how you intend to achieve that. Chastity belts are a little out of date, Rafael, and I'm afraid an embargo wouldn't have much effect on me,' she told him furiously. 'Tell me, does this really have anything to do with the children? Or is it just the idea that someone else appears to have succeeded where you failed?'

Her taunt fell into a combustible atmosphere like a flaming torch. Rafael went satisfyingly rigid, his lean powerful body bracing as he took a sudden backward step, as though he was mentally endowing her with a much-needed line of defence. If he crossed that line, he would either kill her or...make love to her again. Hotly, invasively, unforgettably. An excitement as entirely primitive as his fury flooded her and she was staggered

by the strength of her imagination and her own barbaric
response to the imagery. Clashing with the ferocious intensity of his stare, she suddenly knew that he was completely attuned to her thoughts and her mouth ran dry
and she quailed, abruptly, disorientatingly herself again.

'No...I am not so to be caught.'

'Who the hell wants to catch you?' Sarah lost her head
all over again, shaken more than she cared to admit by
the unwelcome bond of understanding that had surfaced
between them. She lifted a trembling hand to her aching
head. 'I'm sorry.'

'Sorry?' he raged. 'I do not want this sorry!'

His English had gone to hell. His so-expressive hands
moved in a violent arc of frustration and fury and a
treacherous little pang of tenderness stole through her.
She had sunk low in her need to strike back and she was
not very proud of herself. Conversely, she did not want
Rafael to suspect that other reasons might have lain
behind the ease of his conquest. And if ever anybody
had asked for what they had received today, it was
Rafael! Curiosity? Well, if he didn't like what he believed he had discovered, it was entirely his own fault.

Silence sat like a giant concrete block between them.
Heavy, immovable. He was so possessive, so incredibly,
primitively possessive. All these years he had existed
without her and yet still that unreasoning streak of pos-
sessiveness burned in him as fiercely as ever. Once he
had loved her utterly without reservation. He hadn't
minded the burnt offerings on the dinner table. He hadn't
raged over her excessive need for order. Indeed he had
made vague and endearing attempts to be more tidy. He
had bought her flowers, surprise presents...

Disconcertingly tears scorched her eyelids. It had been
so long since she'd allowed herself to remember those
things. But he had also flushed her contraceptive pills
down the toilet when she'd threatened to leave him. He
had also betrayed her in the most agonising way a woman

could be betrayed by someone she loves. And inevitably she thought of the woman in the photograph with her glorious black tumbling hair and sloe-dark eyes. Pain tore into her momentary weakness and pain triumphed.

'Tomorrow afternoon, I fly back to Spain,' he said harshly.

The news swept her with mute gratitude. *'Bon voyage.'*

He strolled soundlessly over to the window and dug a hand into the pocket of his well-cut trousers, stretching the fine fabric tautly over his long, muscular thighs. Her colour heightening, Sarah glanced hurriedly away from him.

'I do not come often to England and at this time it is difficult for me to be away long from my home. My grandmother is very frail...'

Sarah stared at him. 'I didn't know your grandmother was still alive.'

He shrugged. 'Why should you? While my grandfather lived, I had no contact with her.'

'You never told me he was alive either!'

'There was no reason to when I did not visit,' he fielded impatiently. *'Abuela* is an invalid now. I want her to meet her great-grandchildren. I also want to spend time with my children. I want you and the twins to come to Spain.'

Air escaped her lungs in a shocked gush. 'S...Spain?'

'Perhaps you would like me to show you where it is in the atlas.'

'I've already had my holiday leave. It's out of the question,' Sarah told him vehemently. 'We can't possibly come to Spain.'

Rafael dealt her an insolent smile. 'Let me clarify the situation for you. It is really very straightforward. I engaged a lawyer this morning. He believes I have an excellent case. If you don't come to Spain, I instigate court proceedings. Do not underestimate my determination,

Sarah.' The warning was a stark threat in the sudden stillness. 'I want my children.'

Her defiant stance had perceptibly shrunk. Her hands knotted anxiously together. 'It doesn't have to be a fight. I said I'd be reasonable. Unless you're talking about a short week-long visit...' she suggested grudgingly.

'Sarah,' he interposed. 'I expect you to move to Spain.'

'Move to Spain? You've got to be out of your mind! I have a job——'

'Resign,' he slotted in succinctly. 'Give up this place and pack.'

Sarah shook her head, unwilling to believe that he could be serious. 'I'm not leaving England. This is my home.'

'No child of mine will be raised as I was raised.' His dark features were implacable. 'For both of us it will mean sacrifices. Children have very basic needs. They require a mother, a father and a conventional home and I intend to supply each and every one of those needs!'

'In an ideal world! And you may not have noticed but this is not an ideal world!' Sarah threw back furiously.

'They also require love, commitment and discipline. My children,' Rafael stressed, 'deserve to have all of these things.'

'You can visit them!'

'Visit?' He vented a raw expletive. 'That is not enough. Already I have lost four years. And for them there will be no divided loyalties and no insecure worries about where they belong. In short, there will be no divorce.'

'No divorce?' Sarah repeated in rampant disbelief.

'I never gave my consent for a divorce.' His eyes glittered over her angrily. 'Never did I even consider giving it.'

'I don't need your consent!' Sarah exploded. 'In three months I'm having my divorce and you're history!'

Long fingers enclosed her fragile wrist, propelling her forward. Her hair flew back in silk butterfly wings from her shaken face. 'There will be no divorce,' he intoned fiercely. 'Unless you are prepared to lose your children. If you proceed with the divorce, Sarah, I will take everything from you. As once you took everything from me.'

Panic made her limp in his strong hold. 'Rafael...'

A taunting fingertip trailed a sensual path to the valley between her heaving breasts. Predatory black-lashed golden eyes roved over her in an abrasively masculine appraisal before returning to grip her shocked gaze. She shuddered as she felt her flesh tauten and swell where his hand lightly rested in a chemical reaction far more powerful than any force of will. His breath feathered in her hair. 'I could become addicted to torture, *gatita*. You are so incredibly receptive. I can make the hot blood race through your veins. I can make you cry my name in an agony of desire...'

His rich dark drawl had sunk to an intimate whisper that was disturbingly hypnotic. She could taste threat in the air and her throat convulsed but her skin was damp and her rebellious body was responding with anticipation rather than distaste.

'Stop it,' she mumbled thickly.

'I used to dream of what it would be like for you to want me as I wanted you.' His expert mouth located a sensitive hollow above her collarbone. Luxuriant black hair brushed against her cheek and she was swallowed up and swept away by a tidal wave of shivering weakness. 'I would have died for a tithe of what I received this afternoon, but you knew that, didn't you? You gave yourself carelessly, lightly, when you would not give yourself in love. You wanted me to know just once what I had never had. How can I be so ungrateful for this generosity? I shall tell you why. I am not reasonable. I am not liberated. I am not forgiving. Do I apologise for these flaws? Does a man rebel against what is in his blood? Do you think it will hurt more if I don't touch you or if I do?'

She attempted to yank herself free but he held her fast in a grasp of steel, laughing softly now that he had deliberately released her from the spell of his intense sexual magnetism. She was trembling in aftershock from his sensual assault and Rafael's effect on her now was, she registered with a belated surge of understanding, not really that surprising.

She was no longer the mixed-up, repressed young girl she had been five years ago. The combined results of Rafael's infidelity, her father's treatment and those awful weeks shut away with only her own thoughts for company had been traumatic. Harsh circumstance had forced her out of her shell and taught her self-reliance.

She had had to get away from both Rafael and her parents to develop into her own person, to make her own decisions and inevitably her own mistakes. The experience had changed her out of all recognition. She had learnt to handle her emotions openly and without apology. She met with Rafael these days on terms of equality.

She didn't feel threatened or diminished by his extreme masculinity now. She didn't resent his dominance. Rafael could never dominate her now to the extent he had when she was eighteen. As she had grown to like and understand herself, inhibitions grounded on ignorance had gradually fallen away, but Rafael had left her with no desire for sexual experimentation with other men. The sensations and feelings that swept her out of control in his arms stemmed from responses that had once been buried deep and denied.

His hands slid caressingly down over her arms and then dropped away, leaving her feeling strangely bereft. 'I think you should put on some clothes. I've promised to take the children to McDonald's.'

From the sublime to the ridiculous, that was Rafael. He studied her with gleaming amusement. 'I'm not coming with you!' she snapped.

'They would be nervous of me if I took them out alone. You will accompany us if I have to dress you myself.'

'Just try it and see where it gets you!'

'Mummy, are we going out soon?' Ben asked gravely from the doorway.

The trip to McDonald's was a great success. A triangular love-affair was blossoming right under Sarah's nose. She was the intruder, the odd one out. The twins were enthralled by Rafael and Rafael was as gifted at amusing them as he was at keeping their excitement under control. A fourth participant was not required.

Reckless didn't feel so good any more. Her Dutch courage was gone. Her conscience was in death throes. She had enjoyed pleasure for pleasure's sake, and now she was paying the price. Rafael had not made love to her. He had had sex with her. He had cruelly divested the encounter of all sentiment, shredding her foolish dreams with the efficiency of a threshing machine. He had used her. And of one fact she was now certain: he would never receive an opportunity to do so again. She would be ice. She would be so cold he would risk frostbite if he attempted to repeat the experiment.

'Sarah.' A lazy hand caressingly swept a straying tendril of hair back behind her small ear and her heartbeat hit the Richter scale as she clashed unprepared with tawny golden eyes. He withdrew his hand calmly. 'We're leaving,' he said prosaically.

CHAPTER SIX

THE twins slept practically before their heads touched the pillow. Rafael made some quite unnecessary last-minute adjustments to Ben's duvet and picked Gilly's teddy up off the carpet to restore it to the bed. Sarah switched out the light abruptly, determined not to be disarmed by the unashamed tenderness he could display when he chose to do so.

'I have missed so much,' he breathed with regret.

'Yes,' Sarah conceded grudgingly.

'You didn't tell them that I was dead. For that surprising restraint I am grateful but they know nothing about me.'

'What did you expect? A little shrine in the corner?' Sarah was sharply defensive.

He stared down at her with infuriating perception. 'You don't want to share them. That is not generous but I suppose it is human.'

'Thanks for nothing!'

'Sarah.' Lean hands came down on her tense shoulders. 'They are not my children or your children. They are our children. We are not in competition.' It was a reprimand, cool and incisive as only Rafael could make it. 'I did not exclude you this evening. You excluded yourself.'

'You're a tough act to follow.' She headed into the lounge although she wanted to sag and weep with mental and physical exhaustion.

'I liked you better without your barriers. You told me more about yourself over lunch than I learned in two years of marriage. It was not all pleasure.' His beautiful mouth twisted. 'But it was educational.'

He was lounging on the threshold with the supple grace of a wild animal, master of all he surveyed. Leashed vitality still emanated from him in waves. When she looked at him, she felt like a woman was not supposed to feel in these days of equality. She felt weak and feminine and breathless.

Forcing her attention away from him, she drew in a deep breath. 'Look, I'm prepared to come to Spain for a few weeks——'

'It is not enough. It would never be enough,' he dismissed ruthlessly.

'You're telling me to give up my job and my home and tear up my roots just for your benefit? You're being horribly selfish,' she accused shakily.

'Don't make me fight you, Sarah.' Fierce dark eyes without a hint of warm gold rested on her. 'Don't make me do something we will both regret. I want what is best for Ben and Gilly. I have no wish to deprive them of their mother or to deprive you of them. So, you and I . . . we must make a compromise.'

A shard of savage pain seized her. 'I don't like compromises.'

His strong dark features were taut. 'I have never made one before. I do not want this one but I see no alternative.'

'You haven't even given yourself time to think about what you're doing!' There was a desperate edge to her trembling condemnation.

'I knew,' he contradicted very softly. 'I knew, I think the very first night, what I would do but I fought it. I was still up at dawn. I made myself remember how it once was between us. We were both very young, *es verdad?* I expected too much and gave too little. Also...' he spread lazy hands but the brilliant driven emotion in his eyes negated the careless gesture '... I am not very good at loving someone who does not love me.'

'Oh, for pity's sake!' Sarah lost all patience, all control. 'Why the hell did I stay with you so long if I didn't? What did you want? A written statement in blood? Don't ask me why but I was crazy about you! I didn't think I'd anything left to live for when you disappeared out of my life!'

'Sarah...' he breathed huskily.

Struggling for breath, she looked at him. He was wearing the most brilliant smile. It slashed his sensual mouth like diamonds in the sunlight and the pulling power of that smile made her tremble, batten down her hatches with the speed of a hedgehog sensing attack. 'I think it's time you were leaving. Suzanne must be ready to send out a search party for you!'

'You still believe that I sleep with her?' She was delighted to see that the smile had gone.

'What I believe has precious little to do with sleeping,' she said acidly.

'I do not do this either,' he returned levelly.

'Never?'

The faintest bar of colour threw his high cheekbones into prominence. 'It...it was a very long time ago.'

Why wasn't she starring in a circus act where someone with a very poor aim threw knives at her? This was how it would feel when cold steel drove out her life's blood. 'While we were married?' she pressed helplessly.

He was very tense. 'I do not want to talk about this, Sarah.'

'I thought you were all for speaking the truth and shaming the devil! Don't disappoint me.'

'*De acuerdo.*' He expelled his breath in a hiss. 'It was after we parted, after I received your demand for a divorce...'

Hatred was a poison spreading within her. She was in a passion of pain. She wanted him struck down by lightning and retribution, punished into oblivion where he couldn't hurt her any more.

'I met her when I was very drunk and very depressed,' he murmured harshly. 'We made better friends than lovers. You wanted a divorce, Sarah. Do not judge me for this.'

'I judged you five years ago and I haven't any reason to change my mind.' Valiantly she lifted her chin although she was dying inside.

'Suzanne's husband, Eduardo, is also staying in my apartment. Their little boy is having an operation at one of your famous London hospitals. He has been very seriously ill and now he is recovering. I offered them my apartment while they were here.'

Sarah gave no sign of having heard a word of his grated explanation. She was still hating him with so much venom that she marvelled that he did not drop dead at her feet. The front door shut with a quiet thud and she sagged and knew she was going to spend another night watching dawn break the dark skies beyond her bedroom window.

The next morning she handed in her notice at work. The personnel officer frowned but said nothing. Her departure would scarcely cause the company to grind to a halt. But Sarah had valued her job and was bitterly aware that in a few months time it would be well-nigh impossible to find another position as suitable. But what else could she do? The risk she would run in allowing Rafael to take her to court was unthinkable. Such a case would attract immense publicity, especially once the facts began emerging. She would be on trial and she could not afford to be put on trial. Thanks to her father she had spent almost two months in a clinic for the mentally disturbed. Who was ever going to believe that she had been put there when there was nothing the matter with her?

And there was still hope, she told herself, that their differences could be settled without resort to the law. Rafael might soon become bored with fatherhood. Gilly and Ben could be extremely demanding and difficult. Where would they be staying in Spain? In his grandmother's home? The set-up would certainly cramp his style. Rafael demanded total seclusion when he was painting and the twins would be constantly underfoot. Patience wasn't one of his virtues. And how could he possibly imagine that they could live together again? Rafael was very hot on sounding off high ideals about how he wanted his children to grow up. Just how good was he likely to be in the field when he found his own freedom curtailed? She could afford to bide her time for a few weeks and let him find out those facts for himself.

When she arrived at the nursery school to pick up the twins, Rafael was standing on the steps talking to their teacher, Gilly clinging to one hand, Ben to the other.

'Gilly... Ben.' Sarah stuck out her hand impatiently.

'We're saying bye to Daddy.' Ben stayed where he was, a truculent cast to his small face. Gilly turned her head the other way and pretended not to have seen her mother.

Descending the steps, Rafael shook them free. 'When your mother tells you to do something, you do it.'

Ben gave him an obstinate look. 'No.'

Gilly tossed her head. 'No.'

Sarah held her breath, awaiting a lion's roar from Rafael. Instead he crouched lithely down on a level with them. 'Why not?'

Gilly's rosebud mouth quivered. 'Peter Tate's daddy went away on a plane and never came back.'

Ben scuffed at the ground with a trainer-clad toe, striving to hide his fear behind a façade of cool. 'Daddies do that all the time, I s'pose,' he muttered.

'I promise that I will not.' Rafael slid his gold watch carelessly off his wrist. 'Soon you will be coming to Spain to stay with me. Will you look after this until you see me again?'

There was an overbright glitter in Rafael's beautiful dark eyes. Sarah glanced away, her throat thickening. Rafael was *sol y sombra*—sun and shade. She had fallen in love with his warmth and his vibrance. In her innocence, she had not begun to understand the dark, savage complexity that lay beneath. By the time she had understood, it had been too late. Rafael had retreated from her. Rafael, once so open with her, had shut her out. She hadn't known how to reach him. She had been afraid to try. She had been so certain that he intended to leave her. She had walked on eggshells for months.

But what if Rafael had been walking on eggshells too? He had wanted her to have a baby. He had ensured that she became pregnant. How many men still wanted a child in a failing marriage? He must have valued their marriage much more than he was prepared to admit at the time. Sudden anger seized her. Why was she thinking like this? What he might have felt five years ago had no bearing on the present.

He didn't have a faithful bone in his body. That woman in New York and the beautiful Suzanne who had followed had been as inevitable as a cold wind on a January day. Passionate affairs, equally passionate partings. And Sarah had too much pride and too much anger still trapped inside her to become part of that pattern. Ice, she reminded herself and ice she would be. Yesterday he had taken her by surprise. Yesterday her own body had taken her equally by surprise. The next time, she would be prepared. The next time, she would freeze.

Rafael joined her at the railings. 'I wanted to see them again before I left,' he murmured intently, employing a long-fingered hand to edge her round to face him.

Sarah slapped his hand away in instantaneous rejection. 'Don't touch me!'

Within view of the children she had thought herself safe but she discovered her mistake. He drew her inexorably into his arms, clamping her slim body to the virile strength of his. He devoured her mouth with hot, compelling urgency, his tongue stabbing between her lips with a piercing sweetness that was as devastating as it was unexpected. She fell into that kiss like ice-cream melting on a hot summer day. When he set her back from him, she staggered against the railings and he steadied her with a mocking hand. 'To be continued,' he promised, tawny eyes blazing with raw amusement.

He strode across the pavement and swung into the taxi waiting by the gates.

'That was disgusting,' Gilly said loudly.

'People on TV do it.' Ben was slightly less censorious but he was obviously embarrassed for her. He could not have been half as embarrassed as his mother was.

Why did the phone or the bell always go when she was in the bath? Sarah snatched irritably at a towel and pulled on her robe in more or less the same motion, wondering who could possibly be at her door at half-ten at night. Karen was in New York. And it certainly wouldn't be her parents. That particular confrontation had taken place four days ago and had she announced that she was running away with a mass murderer she could not have achieved a bigger effect.

It was Gordon on her doorstep. Taken aback, she flushed, recalling that she had refused to see him twice in the last week and had relied on his male ego to make him take the hint without forcing the issue.

'Obviously I've come at a bad time, but do you mind if I come in?'

Reluctantly she showed him into the lounge. He took up a stance by the fireplace, rather pink and stiff about the face. 'I dined with your father at his club tonight,' he said thinly. 'He told me that Alejandro is your husband and that you're going back to him. I couldn't believe what I was hearing.'

'My father shouldn't have involved you.' Sarah sighed.

It was the wrong thing to say. 'Don't you think I had a right to know?' he demanded. 'If you must know, I was damned grateful that your father did choose to take me into his confidence. He's worried sick about you and the children and I'm not surprised!'

Sarah tilted her chin. 'Tell me, did Rafael figure as a wife-beater, a fortune hunter or a womaniser? Or all of the above? I should warn you that my father doesn't limit his imagination.'

'I want to help you, Sarah. He must be putting pressure on you through the children. You can't be doing this willingly,' he asserted. 'You need a good lawyer and I hadn't planned to say this yet but in this situation, well, perhaps I ought to say it. A respectable new husband in the wings wouldn't be a disadvantage either.' He paused, quite instinctively for effect. 'I have been thinking of asking you to marry me.'

His careful wording roused a wicked twinge of amusement in her but it couldn't survive when he was so obviously upset and sincere. 'That's very kind of you, Gordon, but——'

'I'm not being kind.' He gripped her hands before she could back away. 'You don't belong with someone like Rafael Alejandro. You're panicking into the worst possible decision. I can understand that you're angry with your father. Alejandro should have been told about the twins when they were born but after what he put you through I can equally well understand why your father wanted to protect you.'

Sarah turned an angry pink. 'I don't need to be protected from Rafael.' She attempted to break loose when he linked his arms round her but his slim build was deceptively strong. 'Don't,' she pleaded in distress.

'You're actually defending him!' he grasped in disbelief. 'You're not even giving me a chance. I just asked you to marry me!'

He kissed her angrily, forcibly and then he lifted his fair head, reading the annoyance in her pale face. 'I'm sorry, I——'

'Mummy does that with Daddy too.' Gilly was watching them from the hall.

'What are you doing out of bed?' Sarah snapped.

Gilly took one look at Sarah's stern expression and turned and vanished back into the bedroom.

Gordon was straightening his tie, affronted by the interruption. 'When are you flying out?' he asked curtly.

'Day after tomorrow.'

His mouth tightened. 'What is it about him? He's over here less than a week, he snaps his fingers and you run!'

'It isn't like that, Gordon!'

'From where I'm standing it looks exactly like that and if one half of what your father said is true you are riding for one back-breaking fall,' he forecast.

'I didn't ask for your opinion. And you don't really want to marry me, Gordon,' she responded ruefully. 'I can't see you as a stepfather.'

He reddened. 'I do want to marry you and I think you're making the biggest mistake of your life. Your father believes that Alejandro is using you to strike back at him.'

'Rafael isn't that petty.' She was stung into the retort.

'I hope you're right, Sarah. Pawns don't survive long on the board,' he spelt out unpleasantly.

Their flight was delayed and it was late afternoon when they finally landed in Seville. The heat was horrific. By the time Sarah had reclaimed their luggage and dissuaded the twins from wandering off and getting lost, she felt hot and tired and bedraggled.

'Where's Daddy?' Gilly wailed.

Where indeed? Sarah wondered grimly as she scanned the busy reception area. Of course, in the few minutes he had spared her on the phone he hadn't said that he would meet them; she had taken that for granted. It really didn't pay to take things for granted with Rafael.

'Señora Alejandro?'

She spun and found herself facing a portly little man, clutching a chauffeur's cap between his hands. 'Yes...*sí?*' she adjusted uncertainly.

'Don Rafael sends his apologies. He is unable to be here,' he said in slow and carefully enunciated English. 'I am the chofer, Timoteo Delgados. Please to follow, *por favor.*' His expression was anxious, suggesting that he had just delivered a well-rehearsed speech.

Without further ado, he took charge of the trolley and cut a firm passage through the crowds. Gilly and Ben raced ahead and Sarah quickened her pace to keep up. It was cooler outside but the more bearable temperature barely registered with her as she crossed to the parking area. Timoteo was loading their cases into an incredibly opulent white Rolls-Royce. Sarah raised a brow. It had to be a hire car, she decided, and a limousine was decidedly over the top. A personal appearance from Rafael would have been far more impressive.

'Is it a long drive?' Timoteo regarded her blankly. 'Have we far to go?' she rephrased.

'Lo siento mucho, señora. No hablo inglés,' he confided worriedly.

He slammed the door, sealing them into the luxury interior. In a spirit of rebellion Sarah kicked off her shoes and flexed her cramped toes while her highly impressionable children exclaimed over the superior mode of their transport. Even so, she was conscious of a treacherous little jag of excitement when she looked out on the city's narrow, tortuous streets and flat-roofed white houses and glimpsed the Gothic magnificence of the fifteenth-century cathedral that stood out against the

stark azure-blue skyline. Too soon they were speeding
down the motorway where interesting views were at a
premium and it was almost an hour before they grad-
uated on to twisty country roads. Silvery green olive
groves and orchards bursting with oranges and lemons
were interrupted by rich expanses of pastureland. An
evocative citrusy scent filtered into the car and her nostrils flared appreciatively.

The limousine began to slow down at the top of a
steep hill and made a graceful turn into the mouth of a
massive stone archway barred by tall wrought-iron gates.
In electronic silence the gates parted and swept back. A
broad tree-lined driveway stretched straight as an arrow
before them.

Sarah sat bolt upright and stared. The driveway fanned
into a delicate arc in front of a vast building boasting
an elegant façade of slender columns and arches in an
architectural style that was strongly reminiscent of a
Moorish palace. An exotic tangle of red and violet bou-
gainvillaea cascaded over the walls. Stone urns of hy-
drangeas and geraniums in full bloom studded the
mosaic-tiled terrace beneath the arches. Through the trees
she had teasing glimpses of verdant gardens embellished
with palms and fountains playing glittering jets of water
into the hot, still air.

Her frown of astonished incomprehension slid away.
Obviously Rafael had booked them into a hotel. She
should have guessed that at the airport when the
chauffeur and the limousine had materialised! Presumably two weeks' cool-headed reflection had persuaded Rafael that full-time parenting might make
serious inroads into his freedom. And they were only
two and a half months short of a divorce. In London
Rafael had decided too much in the heat of the moment
and this was the result. Bitter anger currented through
Sarah as the car drew to a stately halt. He was a self-
centred, double-dealing swine! He had uprooted her

from her job, her home and her security on a whim, and now he was parking them under a hotel roof where they could cause him the least possible inconvenience!

'Daddy!' Ben squealed, and as Timoteo opened the door the twins hurtled in a miniature stampede towards the male standing on the terrace.

Sarah alighted with a lot less haste, an icy smile on her lips. An enormous amount of hugging and kissing and frantic speech was being exchanged. In a white shirt that threw his gleaming black hair and bronzed skin into prominence and slim-fitting black jeans that sleekly accentuated his narrow hips and the long, lean line of his legs, Rafael looked infuriatingly spectacular.

'Why wasn't you at the airport?' Gilly demanded ungrammatically.

'*Abuela*...my grandmother, she was not well,' Rafael was explaining in suspiciously carrying tones because Sarah was taking her time about joining them. 'But you will meet her tomorrow when she is feeling better. She is very much looking forward to meeting you.'

Red that had little to do with the heat was warming her skin, a flag of guilt for all her unpleasant assumptions as to the reasons behind his failure to show.

'Can we go into the garden?' Ben asked.

'Yes but you stay out of the water,' Rafael decreed. As the twins took off, rich dark eyes zoomed in on Sarah and lingered. 'You look tired. You should rest before dinner.'

'Oh, you're joining us for dinner, are you?'

His winged brows drew together. 'Where would I be going?'

Sarah shrugged. 'I just wondered. I wouldn't want you to over-exert yourself on our account.' He was staring at her, unusually slow on the uptake to the challenge of a thrown gauntlet. She spread an admiring glance over their surroundings. 'Not that I have any complaints. This is a beautiful hotel. As long as you're picking up the bill, I'm perfectly happy to stay here.'

Rafael tautened. 'This is not a hotel, Sarah.' He hesitated. 'This is my home.'

'Your home?' Sarah laughed and then stared at him wide-eyed for a staggered pause, searching his level gaze for some sign of humour and finding none. In the hot and cold limbo of shock, she whispered, 'You're not joking, are you?'

'I would have a strange sense of humour if I were.'

The taut silence was smashed by a loud splash followed by a combined shout and screech. Rafael swung on his heel with a curse and tore down worn stone steps into the gardens. The twins were clambering guiltily out of a lily-pond the size of a swimming pool.

'What did I say?' Rafael roared.

'I wanted to sit on the big leaf,' Gilly howled.

'Rafael...' Sarah interposed.

'Go into the house and cover your ears if you can't bear to hear this!' he shot at her.

He tore strips off them. He explained the danger. He drew an excruciatingly horrible description of death by drowning. By the time he had finished the twins were more chastened than Sarah had ever seen them. The hovering presence of two uniformed maids and an older woman in a black dress, who had come hurrying outside in the midst of the fracas, forced Sarah to keep her tongue between her teeth.

Rafael issued instructions in a flow of Spanish and Gilly and Ben were removed dripping from the scene by the dark-eyed maids, who were trying to hide their smiles. The older woman remained.

'This is my housekeeper, Consuelo,' Rafael murmured smoothly.

'*Buenas tardes, señora.* I hope you had the good journey.' Consuelo's homely face was wreathed with a pleasant smile.

'*Muchas gracias,* Consuelo. I am glad to be here,' Sarah lied shakily.

'We would like coffee in the *sala,*' Rafael dismissed the older woman with an inclination of his dark head. He glanced at Sarah. 'You are angry with me. All the children need is a firmer hand. They have to learn that when I say no, I mean no. When you say no, sometimes you mean maybe, sometimes you even mean yes, please. For myself, I do not mind this indecision; it adds spice.'

Still too shaken even to reply in kind, she followed him silently up on to the terrace where she preceded him through arched balcony doors. With a numbed sense of complete unreality, she walked into a very large and exquisitely furnished room. A stunning Aubusson carpet of beautifully blended pastels lay beneath her feet. Elegant curio cabinets and silk upholstered couches abounded. *Objets d'art* were dotted with negligent ease on polished antique surfaces throughout the room. Everything she saw screamed old-established money and exclusivity, collections gathered up over generations and displayed with often careless understatement.

Rafael's home. How could it be possible? No, she could not believe it yet. She was still fathoms deep in shock. Presumably this treasure house had devolved to Rafael through his father's side of the family. He had never talked about them. For two years of marriage he had kept all this a secret from her. Not a hint, not an accidental single slip had escaped him.

'Why didn't you tell me?' She could no longer suppress the feelings of angry hurt and betrayal warring within her. 'You let me make an outsized fool of myself.' She shook her head numbly. 'I feel humiliated.'

Rafael elevated a brow. '*Enamorada,* that is not the stock Southcott response to hard currency in plenty.'

'I just don't understand how this is possible,' she muttered tightly.

'During our marriage, I was not welcome here at Alcazar,' he advanced with flat emphasis. 'I received nothing from the estate although I was legally entitled to an income from it. My grandfather, Felipe, hated me and I must confess I had no greater affection for him.'

Her brow furrowed. 'He hated you?'

'Early this year, Felipe met his death very suddenly in a car accident. But for that twist of fate, it would have been many years before I came into my inheritance and I would not have come here like a beggar to the gates.' His dark eyes flashed. 'There was no reason for me to boast of what I could not offer you. That is why I did not talk about this before.'

Consuelo entered with a tray of coffee and daintily cut sandwiches.

'I don't want anything,' Sarah mumbled as the housekeeper departed.

'Don't be silly.' Rafael poured the coffee. 'We don't dine before ten.'

'Food would choke me,' she said truthfully. 'I feel more like fresh air.'

Opening the balcony doors with shaking hands, she stepped back out on to the terrace.

'Sarah——'

'How much are you worth?' she asked with deliberate crudity.

He rested back against one of the twisted barley sugar columns. 'I don't know.' He fixed impatient dark eyes on her shuttered profile. 'There is the estate and the commercial interests. Santovenas have always been most efficient at worshipping and doubling the almighty dollar.'

'Santovena,' Sarah echoed.

'The name is on your marriage licence,' Rafael reminded her. 'I swore I would not use it while Felipe lived. I kept my promise.'

Rafael Luis Enrique Santovena y Alejandro. It had been many years since Sarah had had cause to recall Rafael's full name.

'Santo,' Rafael filled in helpfully. 'Santo Amalgamated Industries.'

Sarah went white. She had heard that name bandied back and forth over dinner in business discussions in her parents' home. Santo was a giant multinational conglomerate with one foot in Europe and the other firmly set in North America. To match Rafael to that heritage was like asking her to walk on the moon. Her brain was frankly not up to the feat.

'As Felipe's successor, I am the largest stockholder. If he could have taken his stock with him to the grave, he would have done so.'

'I feel like a walk.' Her voice was stifled, choked as she descended the steps.

She felt sick. Money meant power. Power would be all it took to permanently remove her children from her care. It was astonishing that Rafael hadn't thrown all this at her in London. I have a good case, he had said with what was, in retrospect, nauseating understatement. She could not compete with Santo. She heard Karen's voice that day in her flat. 'Elise told me that he's from a very wealthy background.' Elise must have had access to privileged information. The press had yet to connect Rafael Alejandro with the massive holdings of SAI.

'Dios mío, qué te pasa?' Rafael demanded from one side of her.

What is the matter with you? Was he serious? Was he really serious? Ben and Gilly would never be hers again. Rafael would be calling every shot. Rafael would be laying down the rules, whether she went or whether she stayed. Why me, oh lord, why me? Escaping her father's power and influence had been tough enough. Escaping Rafael backed by the Santo multimillions was beyond the bounds of possibility. She had played right into his hands by coming here and there was no contest now. The battle had been fought and won before she reached the field.

'I expected you to be delirious with joy,' he breathed.

'God, I hate you! Do you hear me? I hate you!' Sarah launched like a virago as she suddenly found her tongue. Planting her hands up against his chest when he attempted to yank her into his arms, she gave him a violent push and watched with no small amount of satisfaction as he went backwards into the lily-pond with an enormous splash that soaked her as well.

'I worried myself sick about money when we were married!' she shouted. 'And you wouldn't even let me use my trust fund! Oh, no, I had to rough it and all the time you had all this behind you! You went out of your way to horrify my parents! You told my mother you were a gypsy! You told her you'd never met your father! How many parents want their teenage daughter to marry a gypsy without a steady job and an attitude problem?'

The water was still. Sarah blinked rapidly. Where was he? Oh, my God, my God. Kicking off her shoes like a maniac, she jumped in. Something slimy brushed against her calf and she shrieked. Rafael surfaced, thrusting his dripping hair back off his brow, unholy amusement glittering in his tawny eyes.

'Y... You pig! You absolute toad! How dare you give me a fright like that!' Sarah raged.

Endeavouring to climb out again was no easy task, hampered by a sodden full skirt. Rafael stepped out and hauled her up, only he didn't put her down again. He swept her into his arms 'If your mother could only see you now, *gatita,*' he chided mockingly.

'You asked for it!' Sarah wasn't backing down but she was shaking with reaction to that last shock, that hideous gut-wrenching moment when she had believed that he might have been hurt and she would have plunged into a ravine if need be to find him.

Rafael was studying her drawn features. 'You look like a *fantasma*—a ghost—and in my arms you weigh like a little bag of bones,' he criticised. 'I don't like skinny women. You have been neglecting your health.'

Sarah shut her eyes on a wave of exhaustion, feeling like an ugly, undesirable toothpick. 'Oh, leave me alone,' she muttered childishly, close to tears.

'You need to rest. *Dios,* Sarah,' he murmured, determined to drive the point home, 'you look terrible.'

He carted her up a long staircase and there was the sound of an opening door, a woman's anxious voice and then silence. She opened her eyes, surprising a purposeful look on Rafael's taut features. He settled her on her feet and she saw the threat in advance. 'I can manage,' she said hurriedly.

'Don't be a prude! You are half dead on your feet,' he condemned, whipping her cerise cotton top over her head and muffling her response. Her skirt dropped to her toes.

'They're dry!' she gasped before he could get a finger near her skimpy undies.

'*Bueno.*' He lifted her and settled her down on the bed, hauling the tapestry bedspread unceremoniously over her. 'Go to sleep,' he urged.

Winded, she lay back while he drew the curtains. She was on a bed the size of a football pitch. That was all she had time to notice before the shadows folded in. She would lie still until he left. She wasn't that tired. In two minutes, she would get up again.

CHAPTER SEVEN

A LIGHT knock on the door awakened Sarah. Consuelo entered quietly, switching on a lamp a considerate distance from the bed before smilingly producing her robe. Sarah got up, spreading a dazed glance over the magnificent appointments of her room. She explored through a connecting door to find a fully fitted dressing-room, adjoined by a bathroom that contained an exotic sunken bath covered with tiny multicoloured mosaic tiles. Alice through the looking glass could not have felt more disorientated. The feeling was reinforced when Consuelo reappeared with a maid in tow.

'This is Pilar, *señora*. She is learning the good English,' Consuelo proffered cheerfully. 'I hope she will be satisfactory.'

'*Muchas gracias,* Consuelo.' Sarah couldn't think of anything else to say. A maid? What was she supposed to do with a personal maid? Her parents' staff consisted of a housekeeper, a cook, a gardener and a cleaner who came in daily from the village. There had never been a maid.

'*De nada, señora.*' Consuelo beamed.

Sarah asked where her clothes were and Pilar shyly showed her into the dressing-room. Sarah extracted a sapphire-blue dress and with an apologetic smile vanished into the bathroom. It was half-nine and she wanted to see the twins before she went down to dinner. She eyed the bath and the shower regretfully and made do with a refreshing wash before renewing her light make-up and brushing the tangles out of her hair.

124

Pilar had not been idle during her absence. The bed was made and her discarded clothes were gone. Pilar was arranging one of her nightdresses with touching care across the smooth bedspread. Its polycotton simplicity did not lend itself to display.

'Are the children downstairs?' Sarah enquired.

'I will take you to them, *señora. Los niños,* they are in bed.'

Her daughter was sleeping like a royal princess in a canopied bed flowing with lace draperies. The room had clearly been freshly decorated; the furniture was child-sized and more toys than Sarah had ever seen in one place outside a toyshop filled up every available corner. Across the corridor, Ben lay dead to the world in a miniature racing car bed.

'I have four years to make up.' In a superbly cut white dinner-jacket and narrow black trousers, Rafael looked arrestingly like a Spanish hidalgo as he crossed the carpet to join her. 'I don't want to spoil them but I wanted to buy them everything I saw,' he confided, a slight roughness to his deep voice. 'Perhaps I bought too much but I thought these things would help them not to feel homesick.'

'Homesickness doesn't usually flourish in the children's version of paradise. It won't do them any harm this once,' she allowed. 'I'm underdressed, aren't I? I'm afraid I didn't bring anything long with me.'

'You didn't bring many suitcases either. *No importa,*' he dismissed. 'You can buy more clothes.'

There was a distance about him, an aloof quality that hadn't been there earlier, but it was absent when he stared down at Ben as if he still couldn't quite get over the fact that he was a father. She had misjudged him. He was not about to duck the commitment he had promised and it must have been wishful thinking when she had thought he might. Rafael was as unashamedly enthralled with the twins as they were with him and he was sufficiently masculine to see no reason to hide how he felt.

At the head of the curving marble staircase, he abruptly grasped her hand. 'Where's your wedding-ring?' he demanded.

'I don't have it any more.'

Rafael gazed down at her incredulously. 'What did you do with it?'

'I gave it to Oxfam. A good cause, you'll agree.'

'You gave it away?' he repeated thunderously. 'What sort of a woman gives away her wedding-ring?'

'The sort who doesn't attach very much importance to it,' Sarah supplied with spirit and continued on down the stairs.

His strong jawline clenched. 'I will buy another ring and you will wear it at all times.'

Sarah threw back her head. 'If it's so important I'll wear one, but please don't embarrass me with anything flashy. It may have escaped your notice, Rafael, but I have been divorcing you for the past four and three quarter years. It's been a very long time since I thought of myself as a married woman.'

Anger had sparked flames of gold in his eyes. 'That, too, I can do something about.'

A slightly built young man was standing with a drink in the *sala*. With a distinct sneer on his handsome features, he raised his glass high as they entered the room. 'Allow me to toast the blushing bride.' He spoke with a noticeable American accent.

'Sarah has been my wife for nearly seven years.' Icy, unvarnished reproof steeled Rafael's retort. 'Sarah, this is my cousin, Hernando Santovena y Alvarez.'

'*Bienvenido,* Sarah,' Hernando drawled mockingly. 'Rafael misunderstood me. I only meant that to my family you are still a bride. We learnt of your existence only last week. Rafael has such a very short memory where your sex are concerned. Why, only a month ago——'

'*Bastante!*' Rafael silenced him with raw contempt. 'You are drunk. You offend.'

Hernando held up a wavering hand of reproach and drained his glass. 'Say no more. I'm not staying.' His air of forced mockery had been quenched. He looked at Rafael with unconcealed loathing. 'I have no stomach for Consuelo's celebration dinner. What do I have to celebrate?'

Rafael shocked her by smiling with hard amusement as Hernando stalked out of the room. 'One down, two to go,' he quipped. 'What would you like to drink, *gatita?*'

'Gin and bitter lemon.' She frowned at him. 'What was that all about?'

His mouth twisted sardonically. 'It is not very complex. But for my cruel advent into this world, Hernando's father would have inherited on Felipe's death. Hernando grew up looking on me as a usurper and an intruder. The news that I have already fathered a male heir has come as a final, devastating blow,' he delivered with cruel irony. 'There is now no hope of either Hernando or his father ever reclaiming what they still like to believe should have been theirs.'

'But how can they believe that?' Sarah probed. 'You came here as a child.'

He dealt her a grim smile. 'I am the son of a gypsy. For Felipe, my very existence was an insult to the family name. He never accepted me. He spent more than ten years struggling to disprove the legitimacy of my birth. His crusade to disinherit and disown me gave Hernando and his parents false hope.'

Sarah was appalled. 'You were only a child.'

Rafael passed her a crystal glass. 'But you must remember that the stakes were very high. Had Felipe succeeded, he would have made a very generous settlement on me. In victory, he would not have been uncharitable. The Santovenas are a very rich and very conservative family with immense pride in their pure blood lines and a strong belief in the hereditary factor.' He smiled. 'How do you think Felipe felt when he was presented with me?'

'You were still his grandson!'

'But he had washed his hands of my father before I was even born,' Rafael said drily. 'My father was the bad apple in the family barrel. He was a drunk and a womaniser and a gambler, and that is to mention his most presentable flaws of character.'

'That shouldn't have made any difference. Your father was dead!' Dear God, what a horrific childhood he must have had! After his mother's desertion, he had been rejected all over again by his father's family. A family who had had neither poverty nor ignorance to excuse their behaviour. Involuntarily her eyes were stinging with tears. Her surroundings ebbed in their seductive attraction. In this beautiful house, Rafael had suffered.

A taut forefinger feathered over the glistening moisture on her lashes. 'So much heart, *amada*. You fascinate me. Where was your heart when I gave you mine?'

Snatching in a shuddering breath, she did not trust herself to speak.

He dropped his hand. 'I was very much a romantic. I loved you the same moment I saw you. It took more than a moment to forget you again.' His half-smile was derisory, whipping with the cutting sting of a lash over her pain-filled amethyst eyes. 'But it is in the past and I do not pine for it. My soul was no longer my own and in my heart I need to be free. As long as you keep that in mind, ours should be a very civilised marriage. Properly bloodless. I no longer cherish a burning desire to share your every waking thought. That should make you more comfortable.'

Sarah had gone very pale. 'It makes me feel anything but comfortable. It's a recipe for disaster. I came here for the children——'

'Don't be a martyr, *gatita*. I have no time for martyrs,' Rafael warned. 'Here you are at last in the heartland of your most ambitious expectations. The jewel set to a fitting frame. I am certain that even Mama and Papa could be prevailed upon to set aside their prejudice and visit. So don't talk of disaster. All this and family approval too?'

Rafael could be cruel, very cruel when he wanted to be. And she had not been wrong in noting his change of mood from her arrival. Before she could consider that knowledge more deeply, the sound of voices infiltrated her self-preoccupation, sending her attention to the door.

'Sarah—allow me to introduce you to Hernando's parents, my uncle and aunt,' Rafael drawled. 'Ramón and Lucía.'

Lucía was tall, blonde and very thin. Her blue eyes were cold as gemstones and hard as the diamonds that glittered at her throat. Ramón was broad-built and stocky with a heavily lined face and an over-hearty manner. Sarah's arrival was acknowledged by Lucía with the barest minimum of either interest or politeness. Ramón made sporadic attempts to ease the tension with inconsequential remarks. Rafael made no effort to chat at all. The chill of bitter antipathy that kept the conversation stilted was daunting. It was a relief when Consuelo announced dinner.

They took their seats in a splendidly proportioned room, enriched by a dramatic colour scheme of scarlet and gold. The long table might have been set for a banquet. Heavy silver candelbra and old crystal vied with a superb dinner service for prominence.

'I'm surprised that Caterina is not here,' Lucía said sharply.

'She is working round the clock on her next collection,' Rafael murmured evenly. 'The career of a fashion designer is a precarious one. *Abuela* understands this.'

'I am her mother and I do not understand.' The look Lucía dealt Rafael was venomous. 'Caterina has become a stranger to us and you are to blame.'

'I do not think——' Ramón interceded with a weak smile, but what he did not think was to remain a mystery, for Lucía simply talked over him.

'You're the one who destroyed her marriage. You encouraged her to leave Gerry,' Lucía accused brittly. 'Now you finance her so called career. Whatever Caterina wants, Caterina receives, *es verdad?*'

'It is indeed a new sensation for her to enjoy.' Rafael's smile was sardonic.

'My poor Hernando does not meet with this generosity.' Lucía was becomingly increasingly strident.

'I will not preach nepotism to the board for Hernando's benefit.' Rafael turned to address Ramón, indicating that the subject was closed.

Lucía was not to be silenced. 'We are returning to New York tomorrow.'

'*Abuela* will be disappointed,' Rafael responded expressionlessly.

'It is excitement, not disappointment that is dangerous for her.' Lucía smiled coldly at Sarah. 'Your arrival almost killed her. I wonder why.'

'Lucía,' Rafael breathed. 'You may insult me but not my wife.'

'*Por qué?* Will you put a curse on me if I disobey?' Lucía surveyed Sarah with cruelly amused contempt. 'Beware. Rafael is more gypsy than Santovena. He used to light a candle before he would get on a plane. Gypsies are very superstitious, very backward. They live by lies and deception. Education, as you must see with Rafael before you, is wasted on them.'

'Yours didn't do much for you,' Sarah commented before she could bite back her spleen.

Unexpectedly, Rafael flung back his dark head and laughed with rich appreciation. 'Beware, Lucía. My wife is not so quiet as she looks.'

Ugly colour lit Lucía's gaunt bone-structure. 'Why do you not thank us for what we did for Rafael?' she demanded of Sarah. 'When he came to Alcazar he was a dirty little savage. He stole food and hoarded it like an animal. He was violent, he threatened me with a knife——'

'Because you beat me.' Rafael said it so very softly that Sarah almost missed the insertion. His aunt's face set into a blank mask. He lifted his wine glass. 'I believe we have heard enough of the civilising of the little savage. Save it for your charity conventions, Lucía.'

The older woman rose abruptly to her feet. She said something vicious in her own language, flung down her napkin and stalked out of the room. Silence spread in her wake. Ramón stood up, flushed and tight-mouthed. 'I must offer you both my most fervent apologies. *Madre's* illness has put Lucía under great strain,' he proffered without conviction. '*Perdónme* but I must go to her. *Buenas noches.*'

'*Buenas noches,*' Sarah managed, noting the almost pleading slither of Ramón's sad spaniel eyes in Rafael's direction.

'*Buenas noches,* Ramón.' There was an ironic edge to his intonation.

The scene had upset Sarah. Her stomach had taken a nasty somersault when she'd finally appreciated that Ramón and Lucía were the aunt and uncle once given the responsibility of bringing Rafael up. Ramón was weak, utterly beneath Lucía's controlling thumb. And Sarah had seen more than malice in Lucía's eyes, she had seen cold hatred. Her imagination shrank from picturing an embittered Lucía thrust unwillingly into the role of substitute mother. Conscious that she herself was shaken, she glanced searchingly at Rafael. Resting indolently back into his heavily carved chair, Rafael had the slumbrous attitude of a well-fed tiger.

'You could have been kinder to Ramón,' she heard herself say.

'Why? He can control neither his wife nor his son. He should not have brought Lucía here,' Rafael countered. 'Do not mistake his loyalty. Ramón is very much Lucía's satellite.'

Sarah chewed uneasily at her lower lip. 'Evidently your cousin Caterina is the only member of the family to fall into a different category.'

'*Sí*. Caterina and I are very close.' Dark eyes rested on her impassively. 'We are sure to see her before the end of the summer.'

Tension fuelled by sudden suspicion was a steel wire through her body. She was ashamed of the direction her thoughts were taking and suddenly keen to escape Rafael's disturbingly acute scrutiny. 'It's late and it's been a very long day. I think I'll go to bed.'

Rafael smiled, a lazy smile that nevertheless had some elusive quality that increased her unease. Before she could rise, he murmured, '*Momento,* Sarah. I have a sudden desire to hear about Gordon. Don't rush away.'

'What about Gordon?' To her annoyance, she sounded defensive, and then the proverbial penny dropped and her complexion stained with colour. 'I gather Gilly has been chattering.'

'Did you sleep with him that night?' The question was flicked at her with the utmost casualness.

'I'm surprised you didn't grill Gilly about that as well!'

'*Cristo,* what sort of a father do you think I am?' he demanded with raw distaste. 'I questioned her about nothing. It was she who questioned me. She was disturbed by what she saw and, whatever else you did that night, you should have dealt more sympathetically with the child.'

The development of the dialogue had taken an unexpected turn that Sarah was ill prepared for. 'Perhaps I would have, if I'd known there was a problem, but she was asleep when he left and she didn't mention it to me again! And I've had a lot of other things to worry about over the last few days.'

'*Bueno,* but I still await an answer to my original question,' Rafael breathed impatiently. 'You could not give me a straight reply. That is always your way, Sarah. The truth is either to be avoided or ignored. I tell you now, that is not how this marriage will work this time.'

Sarah was angry, hurt and confused all at the same time. 'Do you think I did?'

He did not pretend to misunderstand her. 'You might have done. Angry women are not always wise in the methods of retaliation they employ. You were very angry with me and if he was already your lover I would not say it was beyond the bounds of possibility.'

Sarah was furious. 'Thank you for the vote of confidence! I'm not in the habit of using my body to strike back at another man. And Gordon is not and has never been my lover.'

'*Muchas gracias, gatita,*' he murmured gently. 'Did that hurt so much? *Esta bien.* We have disposed of Gordon. This is fortunate. He was not a very interesting individual.'

Sarah stiffened. 'He wants to marry me.'

Rafael shook her by bursting out laughing. He studied her quizzically. 'A more unlikely candidate for bigamy I have yet to meet.'

'I don't find that particularly funny,' she said tartly, although she had to fight to keep her mouth compressed. 'I'm going to bed.'

His black spiky lashes cast tiny shadows on his hard cheekbones in the candlelight. 'Would I keep a woman from her bed?' he mocked.

Sarah climbed the magnificent staircase slowly, still reeling from Rafael's volatile ability to swing from brooding cool to sudden amusement. She was annoyed when Caterina swam back into her thoughts like an albatross in search of a neck. He was close to his cousin... well, why not? He must have been grateful to have one friend in this household.

In the forlorn hope of distracting herself, she decided to take advantage of the decadent bath adjoining her bedroom. After her nap earlier, she wasn't tired enough to retire to bed. As she slid into the caressing warmth of the water a little while later, her rebellious thoughts marched on.

Lucía loathed Rafael. Could money alone create such sheer hatred? By any normal standards, Ramón and Lucía were very rich in their own right. Had Lucía been exaggerating when she accused Rafael of destroying her daughter's marriage? Could Rafael and Caterina have had an affair? Or was she becoming paranoid? Paranoid was highly probable, she conceded in self-disgust. Look at the fuss she had made about Suzanne! The lady's husband had been in residence as well. At the time the information had been a minor consolation but in a cooler frame of mind Sarah knew that she had no right to question Rafael's lifestyle when she had severed their relationship by embarking on a divorce.

Unfortunately reason and actual feelings, she discovered, were frequently a very poor match. The thought of Rafael with another woman hurt her unbearably. It was a gut response and not one she wanted to feel. For so long she had lived with loving Rafael but when he had been out of her life that love hadn't threatened her, it hadn't made any demands of her, and she had been one step removed from the pain in her detachment. But it wasn't like that now. Emotion was controlling her and unless she was very careful it would betray her again as it had in London. And tonight she felt vulnerable, very vulnerable.

Never again would she need to wonder why Rafael had no respect for family connections and why he had not understood her own conflicting loyalties. He had come here at seven years old and from that day on he had been fighting for survival in an enemy camp. The Santovenas could never have been anything but a threat to him and in the light of what she now knew it was hardly surprising that he had made not the smallest attempt to improve her parents' view of him. He had had no time for them at all and it was that utter indifference which had so enraged her father.

But then Charles Southcott was very small beans to a male who had grown up against a backdrop like this, she acknowledged, annoyance licking through her again. If anything, Rafael had taken pleasure in emphasising his total unsuitability as a husband.

'Not in bed yet?'

She hadn't heard the soft click of the door and her eyes flew wide. In a single driven movement, she leapt upright and grabbed a towel, hauling it frantically round her dripping body. 'Get out of here!'

Hot golden eyes were wandering slowly and quite unashamedly over the gleaming wet curves exposed by the inadequately sized towel. 'Sarah...' he breathed huskily in an entirely different tone as he leant back against the door to close it. 'Stay where you are.'

She scrambled out of the bath. 'Open that door!'

In answer, Rafael shrugged fluidly out of his jacket, letting it lie where it fell in open challenge. An impatient hand reached up to jerk loose his bow-tie, an explicitly intent quality to his heated gaze. 'I have dreamed of you in that bath...'

'I'm warning you, Rafael.'

'Of what do you warn me?' He dropped the tie and embarked ruthlessly on the studs of his white silk dress shirt. 'Surprise me instead. I like surprises,' he murmured provocatively.

'Will you stop taking your clothes off?' Sarah lost her battle for icy dignity and screeched, seriously alarmed when a muscular wedge of bronzed chest sprinkled with black, curling hair swam into view.

'You want me to get into the water clothed?'

'If I were a man, I'd throw you in that bath!' Sarah raged.

The last stud surrendered. 'You do not need to throw me. I come willingly...with enthusiasm,' he stressed.

'I am not sharing that bath with you!'

'You are a puritan. Don't worry. We can overcome this problem.' His sudden slashing grin radiated megawatts of inherent charm and the sort of ruthless determination that took Hannibal over the Alps.

For a split second she was transfixed by the powerful charge of his attraction. For a split second, he could have persuaded her to slow waltz on hot coals. After a staggered pause, she shot back, 'I'm a very angry woman and I want you to leave!'

'To go where?' Rafael was giving the bath a nakedly regretful scrutiny.

'To your own room, where else?' She took advantage of his stillness and slid past him to jerk open the door and move into the bedroom.

'You are in my room. I could always draw a chalk line down the centre of the bed. It would be like old times.'

Sarah swung round and almost overbalanced. 'Your room? I'm not going to share this room with you!'

'You will. We're not having separate rooms,' he asserted fiercely, all mockery banished by the look of horror on her face. 'For years we have lived apart but now we are reconciled——'

'I'm not reconciled with you!' Sarah interrupted furiously. 'I'm not one bit reconciled to what you did to me five years ago and I'm never going to be, either!'

'I have as much cause to feel the same,' he countered harshly. 'But of what profit is it to us now? Sex is not a weapon, *gatita,* and I will not allow you to use it as one.'

Beneath her enraged stare, he strode back into the bathroom. Sarah dropped the towel and dived for her nightdress, feeling decidedly less exposed within its full-length folds. The early hours of the morning were not the best time for a confrontation. Tomorrow she would speak to Consuelo. No way was she sharing this room. And as for that bed? Birds would be singing in the heat of hellfire before she repeated that fatal error! Her attention fixed on the well-padded chaise longue to the left of the window. She trailed the bedspread off the bed and returned for a pillow.

Fury sparking through her, she battered the pillow into shape and curled up in her makeshift bed. How dared he make advances to her after what he had said in London? How dared he? Dear God, what did it take to satisfy him? They were here in Spain. Wasn't that enough? She was reluctant to recall the ominous threats he had made in her apartment. He could not in cold blood drag her into that bed. In fact nobody was more aware than she that a marked lack of enthusiasm was all it took to hold Rafael at bay. There had to be certain ground rules in a situation like this and Rafael had to be made to realise that.

She had come here under pressure. On her terms, she had made a lot more than a compromise. Nowhere had she seen it underwritten that with their arrival a marriage that had fallen apart years ago was suddenly to be resurrected from the dead, regardless of how she felt about it! So much for the properly bloodless relationship he had talked about! It was her considered belief that someone of Rafael's temperament had about as much hope of observing proper behaviour as an alien set down on planet earth.

Sex...she hated that word, hated the casual connotations she could not help attaching to it. Well, she was not a casual person and it was about time he realised that. Just because something that had always gone wrong had miraculously gone right in London was no reason to commit herself to a repeat experiment.

He reappeared, naked but for a carelessly knotted towel hung low on his lean hips. If all else failed, she reflected abstractedly with a suddenly dry mouth, she could always just sit and look at him. Caught red-handed on what was a very sexist thought, Sarah was both amused and shocked by herself. It belatedly occurred to her that in a funny way she was enjoying herself in this battle of wits. And since Rafael did not have a naturally modest bone in his body she read the towel as both concession and retreat.

A second later, she appreciated her mistake. Rafael bent down, scooped her up and dumped her back on the bed. He sent the towel sailing through the air and pinned her flat when she attempted to get up again.

'That is a hideous nightdress. It would repel nine out of ten men,' Rafael pronounced thoughtfully. 'But I am still seeing you in the towel, that so very small towel. This is wasted on me.'

Resentment hurtled through Sarah. Rafael wasn't playing fair. She could not fight his superior strength. 'Is holding me down on a bed one more interesting facet of what you called a civilised marriage?'

'Sarah,' he reproached. 'Surely you do not expect me to be civilised twenty-four hours out of every day? You told me you were a reasonable woman.'

'This is not my idea of a relationship, Rafael.'

'But we are still finding this relationship,' he pointed out speciously.

'All right, if you want it in simple English, I am not in the mood for another experiment!' she snapped.

'Tonight...' His thumb moved caressingly over the sensitive inner skin of her wrist '...we make love, we do not experiment, and tomorrow, I paint.'

'P...paint?' Involuntarily, Sarah seized on the irrelevancy.

His dark head swooped down, his mouth pressing hotly to the tiny pulse flickering crazily beneath his thumb. 'You have interfered with my concentration,' he muttered absently.

An astonishing shiver of awakening awareness snaked through her lower limbs. It took tremendous strength of will to lie rigid. 'If there was anything heavy within reach, your concentration would be the least of your problems.' But her quip was shaky and indistinct. Something unforgivable had happened to her own concentration.

'I like it when you argue with me.' Rafael gazed down at her with eyes the sensuous shade of wild honey and that treacherous something gave a violent lurch in the pit of her stomach. 'But not tonight.'

Without conscious intent her muscles were losing tension, easing into the gradually lowering embrace of his hard, virile body. Self-discipline slid, awareness creeping in. Her nostrils flared, reacting to the familiar, drugging scent of him and an elusive warmth began stealing through her. 'No.'

'De acuerdo,' he murmured, choosing to misinterpret her entirely.

She stared up at him dazedly and somewhere inside her head a little voice of reason was screaming itself hoarse behind a locked door. Once again she could barely credit what was happening to her. He was barely touching her and her breasts were swelling, heat pooling in her pelvis. He carried her hand to his lips and the tip of his tongue very slowly inscribed an erotic tracery on her palm. It had the most extraordinary effect on her, a low moan breaking at the back of her throat. He brought his mouth teasingly close to hers and let his tongue dip in a single, hungry thrust between her parted lips in a caress that was sweeter than honey, headier than wine and her slender length jackknifed upward, inviting his weight.

'You see,' Rafael whispered softly. 'Alcohol is not necessary.'

CHAPTER EIGHT

RAFAEL rolled sideways, carrying Sarah with him, heat and hunger blatant in the blaze of his eyes as he bound her to him with possessive hands. She could have lost herself in that moment as she slid deeper beneath the powerful spell he could cast. The air between them pulsed with emotional intensity and the unbearable tension jerked up another notch.

'Touch me,' he invited raggedly.

Warmth flooded her cheeks as he found her hand and spread her fingers. 'I can't,' she gasped strickenly.

His mouth scorched hers like a burning brand, demanding and receiving her response, sending little tongues of flame through her weakened limbs. Her hand fanned over his lean, bronzed torso, feeling the wild thunder of his heartbeat and the enticing dampness of his skin. Her nightdress was tangled round her hips, forcing her into contact with his hair-roughened thighs. The muscles of his hard, flat stomach contracted violently beneath her roaming fingers and she jerked her hand away, reviling her own clumsiness.

'*Perdición,*' Rafael groaned as if he was in agony.

His hands bit into her hips, a Spanish curse blistering her ears when he became twisted in the folds of her nightdress. The offending garment was dealt with mercilessly and his urgency melted her bones to water. Connecting with a broad shoulder in the darkness, she pressed her lips feverishly to the lure of his flesh.

Rafael reacted by flattening her to the mattress. '*Por dios,* he did not teach you so much.' Primal satisfaction laced every syllable.

A fleeting frown touched her forehead but she did not quite connect with his meaning. His mouth had found the soft, scented valley between her breasts and all power of thought was cast into oblivion. His tongue laved a taut pink nipple, lingered, circled, teased until her fingers clawed into his tousled hair and he ended the torture, giving her what she mindlessly sought until excitement arrowed a tight, coiling message of need to the very heart of her and her nails dug protestingly into his shoulders.

He lifted his head from her swollen breasts and let his hands shape the achingly tender flesh, making her arch her spine, and sweeping down over her quivering stomach to slide tormentingly against her where she most needed to be touched. The ache inside her was intensifying, the pressure was mounting and the motion of his hand as he delicately explored the moist heat of her femininity made her sob out his name as convulsive pleasure overwhelmed her, spinning her recklessly out of control.

In the moonlight he pulled back from her, totally, magnificently male, and she rejoiced in his virile splendour like an idolatress before a golden god. As he knelt between her parted thighs, he raised her and linked her fingers round his strong brown throat. Leaning forward, he slid his hands under her hips and lifted her, holding her poised above him. With a whimper of shock, her passion-glazed eyes clashed with the savage brilliance of his.

'I want to watch you while I love you,' he breathed fiercely. 'I do not want you to forget who I am.'

A smile as untamed as he was slashed his darkly handsome features as he brought her down, the compulsive heat of his mouth stifling her cry at the powerful surge of his possession. His movements were fierce and elemental, invoking an intensity of sensation that brought her to screaming point. The dance of love was more erotic and more demanding than she had ever dreamt it could be. She was abandoned, divorced from everything but the shatteringly insistent demands of her own body. There was a glorious sense of oneness, of a joining that went beyond the physical as her spine arced in ecstasy and she was engulfed by wave upon wave of shuddering release.

It took her a long time to return to reality. Rafael was no longer with her. He was silvered shadow by the open door that led out on to the balcony. The merest hint of a breeze fluttered the draperies that had been drawn back, cooling her damp skin. She shifted over to the edge of the bed in a sensual, happy daze. 'Rafael?'

'Go to sleep.'

Her darkened eyes clung to his hard-edged profile. 'What are you thinking about?' she whispered.

'You do not want to know.'

She pressed her hot face into a cold spot on the pillow. When he made love to her, the past and the present vanished. There was no thought and no discipline strong enough to withstand what he could make her feel. He knew that now without any shadow of a doubt. Had she possessed the same ability seven years ago, their marriage might have survived.

Silent submission had not been enough to satisfy Rafael. She had not rejected him. In the end he had rejected her. And as the physical gulf had widened between them the misunderstandings had begun to multiply. Dear God, she did not feel equipped to deal with the same situation in reverse. She was stunned by the power he had over her and tonight he had used that power as a weapon against her. Neither her pride nor her principles had protected her. On his terms she had surrendered to a purely physical experience that had nothing to do with the marriage bond and even less to do with sentiment. Did that make him feel good? Her stomach turned over sickly. Did that settle the score for the blow she had once dealt to his ego? But if that was true, where was his triumph? Brooding silence did not suggest satisfaction.

'I do want to know,' she said defiantly.

'It is a most exquisite irony.' Dark eyes flicked from the disordered bed to her flushed face, his meaning explicit. 'I was thinking back through the years. Then this might have saved us . . . not forever, you understand, but for a little while longer.'

'I don't think so.' His cool philosophical attitude chilled her. 'After what happened in New York——'

'It was the tip of the iceberg,' he cut in roughly. 'No marriage can survive without trust and without communication.'

'Your idea of communication was a blazing row. I didn't find it encouraging. As for trust?' she muttered tightly. 'Trust is something that has to be earned.'

'Is it really? I loved you and I married you. What more did you want?'

'Big deal,' Sarah quipped.

'*Sí* . . . yes, for me it was a very big deal; it was the most important commitment I would ever make to another human being.'

'I can remember you strolling in at dawn without a single word of explanation.'

'Did you ask where I had been? No!' he snapped.

'If you're trying to excuse yourself——'

'For what?' he demanded fiercely. 'For stopping to give first aid to the victim of a road crash? For spending hours waiting for *les flics* to take my statement as a witness?'

Sarah had paled. 'You saw an accident?'

'What use is it to talk of this now? It is unimportant.'

It was not unimportant to Sarah. For her that night had been a milestone at the brow of what looked like an exceedingly slippery slope. She could remember the days before her father had taken a flat in the city, the last-minute cancellations, the late arrivals, but most of all she could remember her mother's silence, the absolute insistence on behaving as though nothing had happened. For the first time she appreciated that she had distrusted Rafael long before he gave her any cause for suspicion. Her belief that he would inevitably betray her had been there right from the start.

'Or is it? Now in your eyes we are equal,' he gibed, his eyes glittering intensely over the pale oval of her face. 'You are still my wife though you have slept with other men. But I should not be mentioning this fact when we have lived apart. It is fashionable to cultivate the short memory, *es verdad?* It is conventional to pretend indifference——'

'Rafael——' she broke in.

'Crude and positively medieval of me to be thinking that that beautiful pale skin of yours carries more fingerprints now than a police file!' he completed rawly. '*No me gusta . . .* I don't like it. And don't tell me that I do not have the right not to like it! I still don't like it. I don't accept it. I will not deny what I feel.'

His naked candour was shocking, oddly touching on some level that she flatly refused to probe inside herself. She could not fathom how he did it but guilt was surging up on her out of nowhere. She fought off a compulsion to tell the truth. After all, she had not told a lie in the first place. The ensuing complications were not her responsibility, were they?

'Do you ever wonder how I felt in the same situation?' she enquired unsteadily.

A lean hand made a fierce gesture of repudiation. 'It is not the same! In no way is it the same! You didn't want me any more. You wanted me to leave. You made that clear long before I went to New York.'

How could he have believed that? Was that how he had really felt? Rafael, so strong, so innately sure of himself? She was hit hard by the realisation that he had described exactly how she had felt and thought five years ago. The comparison, resurrecting as it did the anguish of rejection, anger and pain, was very disturbing. It was so difficult for her to believe that Rafael might have experienced anything similar. For so long she had lived with a picture of him swinging on his heel and walking away with little more than a backward glance, relieved to have his freedom back. Only now did she see that that had always been an unrealistic picture. Nobody as emotional as Rafael could possibly be that shallow.

'I'm going out.' Before she could speak, he strode into the dressing-room. Cupboard doors opened and slammed, drawers were rifled. She could see him through the ajar door. He was hauling on a pair of paint-stained jeans. Somebody had obviously made a most praiseworthy attempt to hide them. There was something inexplicably vulnerable about the long, golden-brown sweep of his back. Watching him spurred a curious pain within her.

She sat up and sighed. 'There haven't been any other men.'

A broad shoulder lifted in an infinitesimal shrug of indifference as he pulled on a shirt. *'No importa.'*

'I never said that there were.' Sarah was resisting a very powerful urge to throw something large and heavy at him. 'You thought up the idea all on your own.'

'I think what you wanted me to think.'

'Well, perhaps a part of me did want you to think that for a while,' Sarah confessed awkwardly. 'But I don't want you to think it any more.'

'And I don't want your lies!' It was a contemptuous dismissal.

'For the last time,' she snapped, 'I am telling you the truth.'

He released a derisive laugh. 'You must think me a fool.'

Sarah nodded in furious agreement. 'Yes, I am starting to think that. I'm also beginning to wonder why it should matter so much to you.'

He thrust long fingers through his thick black hair, his strong features hard and taut. 'You would not understand.'

She swallowed hard. 'I could try.'

'But I don't want you to try.'

It was a shock to come up against that brick wall. The door thudded softly shut on his departure and she lay down again, feeling as though he had slapped her in the face. She was shaken, badly shaken by his disbelief. Rafael had never doubted her word before. Rafael had always trusted her and until this moment she had not appreciated just how horrible it felt not to be trusted any more.

She awoke late the next morning to the blinding sunlight flooding through the windows. She had dozed on and off throughout the remainder of the night. Rafael had not returned and she had worked through the stages of annoyance and worry before succumbing to a deep sense of hurt rejection. She felt raw and bruised. Last night, for her at least, had been special, or so it had seemed until she refused to go back to sleep and did what she had never used to do with Rafael when he was in a dark mood—ask questions. Obviously there was an art to such tentative advances, an art or perhaps, she conceded painfully, an influence that she just didn't have.

After showering and washing her hair, she pulled out a matching cerise top and skirt and wrinkled her nose at her unexciting reflection. Funny that it should take her until now to concede that Karen's nagging had not been without cause. Her wardrobe was uninspiring. Very practical, though. Everything went with everything else, everything washed. When had she become so safe and sensible? For a couple of years in Truro she had at least experimented with different styles but after a while the fun had gone out of it and she had had other more pressing concerns. Letitia's illness had taken priority. Her face shadowed at the memory.

Consuelo greeted her in the hall. '*Buenas días, señora.* You would like breakfast?'

A table awaited her in a charming, sunlit inner courtyard. The air was heavy with the scent of roses and hibiscus. A maid brought her brioches and hot chocolate and a bowl of choice fruits. 'Where are the children?' Sarah asked.

'*Los niños* are with Don Rafael in the studio, *señora.*'

This I have got to see, Sarah promised herself, but she lingered over her meal, unconsciously revelling in the first peaceful and leisurely breakfast she had enjoyed in years. Stealing a last succulent grape, she was rising from her chair when Consuelo walked out on to the patio.

'Doña Isabel asks that you visit her, *señora.*' The housekeeper had the uneasy look of someone delivering a royal command. 'In the afternoon, she must rest. You will come now, *por favor?*'

'Of course.' Sarah hid her dismay behind a strained smile. 'I hope that—er—Doña Isabel is feeling better today?'

'She is still weak,' Consuelo responded with warmth. 'But this morning, when the little ones come to see her, she is much brighter than she has been.'

So Gilly and Ben had already met their great-grandmother. Between them Rafael and his staff were making her feel pretty superfluous as a mother. The next item on his agenda would probably be a nanny, she thought tautly. Her close ties with the children would be undermined even more. Was she being unfair to Rafael? Did he regard her presence in this house as permanent? Dully recalling his chilling withdrawal the night before, she decided that she was wise to feel insecure.

Consuelo led her up a rear stone stair and into another wing. It was distinctly different from what she had so far seen of the rest of the house. They passed through a door and the wide, airy spaces and soaring ceilings were left behind in favour of long dark-panelled corridors with uneven floors and walls hung with family portraits which she would have liked to examine. Unfortunately the housekeeper's steps were brisk. Doña Isabel, she deduced, did not like to be kept waiting.

Consuelo rapped lightly on a low-lintelled door. It was opened by a woman in a crisp white nursing tunic and Sarah was ushered in.

'You may go, Alice.' A tart voice emanated from the utilitarian hospital bed so at variance with the elegantly furnished room. 'If I require your services, I'll ring for you.'

The nurse withdrew with pronounced reluctance.

'Come over here where I can see you properly,' Sarah was urged. 'You're standing in the sunlight.'

'You speak very good English.' Sarah spoke the thought out loud without realising it, staring helplessly at the gaunt old lady raking her up and down with faded but sharp blue eyes.

'My father was a diplomat in London for many years,' Doña Isabel informed her. 'Please sit down. People who stand over me make me dizzy.'

Sarah took the chair by the bed and withstood an unapologetically thorough appraisal.

'Rafael is no woman's fool.' There was reluctant approval in his grandmother's critical gaze. 'You look like a lady.'

Involuntarily Sarah smiled. 'Appearances can be deceptive.'

'At my age, I'm not easily deceived,' Doña Isabel responded drily. 'I would like to ask why you parted from my grandson but you are together again with the children. That is all that should concern me.' She paused.

'No doubt you are curious to know why this should concern me. Rafael cannot have failed to have told you how this family treated him.'

Sarah met the challenging stare levelly. 'He hasn't.'

The old lady rested back against the banked-up pillows. The frail hand that gripped the raised bed-rail was the only sign of her tension. 'I must try to explain our behaviour.'

'That isn't necessary,' Sarah said uncomfortably.

'I disagree. I lie here remembering what I did and what I didn't do. My conscience—it troubles me even now,' she admitted grudgingly. 'Once we were a happy, united family. Felipe and I had three sons. One was a blessing, one was a curse and one a nonentity. *Qué?* You speak?'

Sarah moved her head in urgent negative, having stifled a gasp over the blunt maternal dismissal of Ramón. As the sole surviving son, he was no more popular with his parent for lack of competition.

'Antonio was the eldest and we adored him. Toni was like the sunshine...everyone loved him.' Although her attention remained fixed on Sarah, there was a faraway look in the old lady's lined features. 'Toni was irreplaceable...'

As the silence lengthened, Sarah moistened her dry lips. 'And Rafael's father?'

'Marcos.' The sunken eyes shut for an instant as if to ward off images that brought pain. 'He was always in trouble even as a child. He was very jealous of Toni. He cost us a fortune when we were not so privileged as we are now. Felipe could not control him. Yet he had charm, tremendous charm when he wanted to use it. He seduced the girl whom Toni loved. He didn't want her. He did it to hurt Toni,' she shared harshly. 'Marcos liked to break things. Look at Lucía now, bitter, so bitter and unpleasant...poor Lucía. She was passionately in love with Marcos. I still pity her.'

'Lucía?' Sarah prompted, certain she had lost the thread. 'Ramón's wife?'

'Before she married Ramón, she was betrothed to Marcos. He jilted her a week before the wedding,' she shared heavily. 'His behaviour could not be forgiven. Felipe told him to leave and from that day he refused to support him. Two years later, we were informed of his death. He died in sordid circumstances. He had become a dealer in drugs.'

'I'm sorry.' But as Sarah spoke she swiftly met her error in the old lady's daunting stare of aloof enquiry.

'He married the gypsy when he was dying of his injuries in hospital. She was many months pregnant. He married her out of malice.'

'Malice?' Sarah queried.

'Without our knowledge, Toni had had some contact with Marcos. Marcos knew that Toni had leukaemia; he knew that Toni's chances of survival were small and that his child, be it boy or girl, would come before Ramón to take all that should have been Toni's had he lived.' The thin voice was jagged, ravaged by the strain of relating tragedy with proud detachment. 'Toni had a long period of remission. We learnt to hope but it was not to be. He died the same year that Rafael came to us. Perhaps we would have reacted differently had we discovered his existence sooner. But we did not. We knew nothing of the marriage. Rafael was delivered to us like a parcel. He had Marcos's eyes and they accused us. Felipe could not bear to look at him.'

'So you handed him over to Ramón and Lucía.' Sarah felt sick, too sick to hide how she felt. She saw it all now. Lucía, cruelly jilted and humiliated by Rafael's father, Ramón suddenly deprived of his status as next in line by a child nephew.

'Ramón agreed. Someone had to take charge of him,' Doña Isabel said defensively but she could not meet Sarah's pained scrutiny. Her thin fingers tightened convulsively on the bed-rail. 'I was still grieving for Toni. Rafael made me feel guilty. It was easier to turn my back and pretend he didn't exist. Felipe...he was so certain that he could not be Marcos's child...and yet I knew...I knew,' she muttered in a distressed undertone.

Sarah's mouth tightened and she drew in a slow, deep breath.

Her companion cleared her throat brusquely. 'When we understood what had been happening here,' she continued evasively, 'we sent him to boarding school. No, we did not redeem ourselves even then. But he was brilliant at school. In every field, he excelled. He could have done anything, become anyone he wanted to be, and little by little we began to take notice of him.'

'What happened?' Sarah encouraged.

'When he was a child he drew on walls when Lucía wouldn't give him paper. There was never a time when Rafael did not paint,' she confided grimly. 'I believe it was a form of escape for him. We gave him no love and no place in the family and we attempted too late to make him one of us. We failed. We could give him nothing that he wanted but his freedom and that he took for himself. He refused to enter the business world. He defied all of us. I learnt...' the old lady's voice was dragging with exhaustion now '...that it is only with love that Rafael can be held or contained. That is the only tie he will acknowledge and we had not created that tie.'

That assessment had an intimate personal reality for Sarah and it hit her hard. After a long pause, she whispered tightly, 'You understand him,' but Rafael's grandmother did not hear her. Doña Isabel had drifted off to sleep.

The British nurse was waiting outside. Sarah apologised for over-tiring her patient. 'Doña Isabel dictates the length of her own visiting hours,' Alice said wryly. 'I wouldn't dare to interfere without good reason.'

Sarah asked where the studio was and discovered that it was in the grounds. The sprinklers on the velvet-smooth lawns were at rest in the heat of midday. Sarah had a ten-minute walk up a gradually steepening slope of terraces before she reached the encircling belt of acacia trees that bounded the formal gardens. She sheltered briefly within their dappled shadows. From there she could see the stone-built studio with its red-tiled roof. The path that ran to the open door was a mere track through long grass and wild flowers. As she approached she could hear the twins chattering.

Several doors opened off the cool, tiled hall. The studio lay to the left, a spacious extension of the original room with floor to ceiling glass at one end. The facing wall was hung with numerous paintings. The twins were down on their knees fingerpainting on a giant sheet of paper. Rafael was suggesting colours with all the enthusiasm of someone privileged to be sharing in the creation of a major work of art. One of his gifts, she recognised, was an entirely unstudied genius for handling children...and one particularly stupid woman, who loved him. Last night, Rafael had made surrender torturingly and unforgivably sweet. With time and the kind of encouragement she was giving him, how much more damage might he do?

But watching those three dark heads meeting in such unity, she finally understood that Rafael would not be deliberately guilty of anything which might hurt the twins. The children would come first. He had said that from the start. He had also mentioned the sacrifices they would both have to make. And she was one of those sacrifices, wasn't she?

She was an unavoidably necessary component of Rafael's determination to give his children the secure and uneventful childhood that he himself had been denied. And making love to her, she appreciated on a wave of anguished hurt, was just one more practical part of that ambition. Rafael was a very highly sexed male. And he had made a very moral decision. Either he satisfied his needs within marriage or he indulged in a series of affairs. Sneaking around was most definitely not Rafael, nor would such behaviour add to a happy home environment for his children.

She was looking at a reformed rake, handcuffed by conscience to the marital bed. And all that storm and passion expended on her imaginary trail of lovers meant not a thing. It certainly didn't mean that he was jealous or that he was reacting with resentment against the events that had separated them, thereby enabling her to indulge in what he clearly envisaged as a voracious appetite for other men. When you didn't really want someone, you became hyper-critical and dwelt on their flaws. Rafael had seized on her supposed scarlet past with a purpose— it gave him a vent for his frustration. He was feeling trapped and like a wild animal he clawed when you put him in a cage.

Ben saw her first. 'Mummy!' he scrambled up, waving rainbow-coloured hands. 'We had breakfast with Daddy and he's teaching us to swim.'

'We saw fish in a river,' Gilly put in.

'We climbed a tree and a wall . . . a great big wall,' Ben boasted.

Gilly pirouetted. 'Daddy says I'll be even more pretty tomorrow if I stop telling people how pretty I am.' Clearly she hadn't quite grasped the message yet.

'Go and wash your hands now.' Rafael sprang gracefully upright, the worn soft fabric of his jeans flexing indecently taut over his lean, hard flanks.

'You've had a very busy morning,' Sarah remarked.

'They wanted to awaken you. It was by my instruction that you were left in peace.' He was maddeningly attuned to her most petty inner resentments.

'I met your grandmother this morning,' she said hurriedly.

Rafael wiped long fingers clean on a rag. 'What did you think of her?'

'How serious is her illness?'

'She had a stroke after Felipe's death but with therapy and determination she would be able to use a wheel-chair,' he explained. 'However, she has lost her interest in life and the longer she lies in that bed the less chance there is that she will ever leave it again.'

'She seems to be fond of you,' she commented.

'Do you think so? I would say she respects me.' His wide, passionate mouth had a wry curve. 'She lives too much in the past now. Fallen idols and grief have become her sustenance. What did you talk about? Let me guess—Toni? I have often regretted not meeting my late uncle. So much perfection in one human being is rare.'

'You're not very sympathetic, are you?'

He laughed uproariously. '*Abuela* would choke on sympathy!' With amusement dying out of his eyes, he looked incredibly attractive. 'Toni was an obsession with her. She had no time for her other children. She takes precious little interest in the surviving four.'

'Four?' Sarah questioned.

'She neglected to mention my trio of aunts?' He smiled. 'Females stand pretty low on *Abuela's* scale of importance.'

'Ramón doesn't do much better.'

'She despises weakness.'

'Strong people tend to,' Sarah said less evenly. 'You have no time for him either.'

'He is a fool.' Rafael was carelessly indifferent. 'Lucía is not even faithful to him.'

'At least he's loyal.'

'So is a dog. Lucía has no need of a pet. To love without return is a form of degradation,' he breathed contemptuously. 'And in the name of that love Ramón has done much to be ashamed of.'

She could feel the colour draining sharply from her cheeks.

His dark eyes were intent upon her. 'About last night——'

'Oh, let's not have a post-mortem,' she interrupted.

'I stayed here,' he continued in defiance of her dismissal. 'I shouldn't have lost my temper. If I upset you, I'm sorry.'

He didn't look sorry, she thought unhappily. He looked more like someone *trying* to look sorry. It was called papering over the cracks. That was what he was doing. In the future there would be many similar episodes if she stayed. Compromise. Give and take. Charades and civil dishonesty were part and parcel of that. Rafael was not the most likely choice for a diplomatic career but possibly time and practice would improve him.

'Forget it,' she said flatly.

'It won't happen again,' he assured her impressively.

'Of course it will,' she contradicted helplessly.

'Why do you have to make this so difficult?'

'Because you're talking nonsense,' she muttered. 'You're no good at pretending!'

Unmistakable bitterness hardened his bone-structure. 'As to that, you may one day be surprised.'

'I doubt it.'

'I want us to be a family,' he emphasised harshly. 'It is very important that you should be happy here at Alcazar.'

With every word he confirmed her suspicions about his own feelings. In no way was she wanted for herself. Without the children, she had no value whatsoever. 'I'll do my best to sparkle,' she said sarcastically.

His mouth compressed. 'Sometimes, I could slap you!'

'That would be most conducive to my happiness.'

'You know what I meant! It was a saying, not a threat. Are you afraid that you will lose contact with your

parents? All right. If you want to bring them over here
on a visit, you can!' It was clear from his expression
that he considered that a magnificently unselfish offer.
'It is a very big house and I would probably see them
only at dinner. What do you think?' he prompted
impatiently.

'I don't really think you want to hear my answer.'

A smouldering dissatisfaction was awkening in his
tawny gaze. 'I am not very good with people I don't
like.'

'I did notice that over dinner last night,' she said
woodenly.

'But for your sake I would make an effort. Who
knows? Time may have changed your parents,' he
breathed with a brooding lack of conviction.

Dear heaven, this was sacrifice. This for Rafael was
the equivalent of lying undefended on a cold stone slab
with a gleaming knife-point hovering over his heart. He
was ready to make the ultimate sacrifice for his children's benefit, most probably on the mistaken assumption that the twins were very attached to their
maternal grandparents. 'I shouldn't worry, if I were you.
I imagine it will take my father quite a while to come to
terms with your connections with Santo Amalgamated
Industries!'

'*Cristo,* Sarah!' Abruptly, he lost patience. 'You are
being deliberately obstructive. I have apologised for last
night. But you are behaving like a sulky little girl!'

'Perhaps I'm less idealistic about the future than you
are and I should know what I'm talking about—I have
lived with you before!'

'Let me spell my intentions out, then,' he grated.
'Whatever you want, you can have. Whatever you want,
I will try to give you. What more can I offer you?'

She couldn't tell him. Her self-respect might be badly
dented but it was still in existence. She wanted his love,
his trust, his understanding. Only none of those things

was on offer. He had loved her when he was twenty-four but that was a long, long time ago and a century in terms of maturity. In those days, compromise would have been a very dirty word in his vocabulary. Then, it had been all or nothing for Rafael.

That day he had called her from New York and issued his forty-eight-hour ultimatum, he had gambled their entire relationship on the single turn of a card. And a day past the deadline and her failure to put in an appearance, he had picked up that exotic brunette at the gallery and taken her back to his hotel room. Until now she had rigorously avoided seeing that connection. It was perfectly possible that in the heat of anger and wounded pride Rafael had believed that their marriage was over, that she had made her final choice and that that final choice did not include him.

'What happens if you fall in love with someone else?' she asked drily. 'What happens then?'

A spasm of pain flashed through his eyes, pain mingled with some other fierce and dark emotion. Regret? Bitterness? It was there so briefly that she might almost have thought her imagination was playing tricks on her had not a lingering tautness to his facial muscles confirmed the impression that she had hit a nerve.

'That is a very unlikely event.'

Sarah felt numb. Quite accidentally she had jerked a tripwire. She had thrown the question off the top of her head, intending only to disconcert him. He had tripped but she was the one who, to borrow Gordon's terminology, had ridden herself into one back-breaking fall. Rafael was in love with someone else. Someone else, someone else . . . the echo rose to deafening proportions in her head.

Perspiration dampened her upper lip and she turned, pretending an interest in the canvases on the wall when in actuality she couldn't see them. A vast and horrible emptiness was yawning inside her, making her wretchedly aware that in spite of everything that she had been busy telling herself she had been cherishing the hope that sooner or later, he might . . . he might what? Love you again? You weren't even his type the first time around!

Her unseeing gaze focused involuntarily on one of the paintings and without conscious volition she moved closer. Recognition shocked her briefly out of her stupor. A girl in a prim white sundress was sitting on the deep sill of a low window, hands folded, feet neatly placed together. All the cluttered paraphernalia of an artist's studio surrounded her. You could taste her tension and isolation. Her shoulders had a defeated droop; her whole posture radiated misery.

'I did it from sketches,' Rafael murmured softly.

'I look like a dying swan.'

'I think you look lost and unhappy. It is not very good.' His intonation had roughened. 'Next time I paint you there will be no comparison.'

She tensed. 'There won't be a next time.'

'But who thought there would be a next time for us?' he countered mockingly. 'And in Andalucía we say, "Life is much shorter than death." You should think about that.'

CHAPTER NINE

'ARE you awake, *gatita?*'

The inhabitants of a cemetery would have been enlivened by the racket Rafael had made coming to bed. Sarah lay very still, play-acting sleep in the darkness.

'You should be. I made enough noise.' He laughed softly. 'Why are you lying over there? I forgot the time. You should have phoned the studio. *Lo siento mucho,*' he breathed huskily as he drew her inexorably into the strong circle of his arms. 'But better late than not at all, *es verdad?*'

'I'm tired,' she muttered curtly.

'*Dios,* Sarah, the bed is here at any hour. I am not,' he teased.

'You conceited jerk!'

'Is this some game that I am to play? Heads, you want me? Tails, you don't?'

Silently, Sarah slid out of his embrace and rolled over to a cool, uninviting stretch of the bed. She had no sense of satisfaction. The unpleasant thoughts that had been her constant companions throughout the afternoon and evening refused to be shaken off. If he loved someone else, why had he made no attempt to speed up the divorce? Or had he only met her recently? Why had he made love to her that day in London? Was it possible that this other woman was already married and out of reach? Was it possible that she didn't feel the same way? For hours, she had tortured herself with every feasible possibility in search of answers that she didn't really want to find. For hours, she had been waiting for him to put in an appearance.

And then what did he do? He strolled in as if he hadn't a care in the world and reached for her as if she was his

160

by some holy, unwritten law. Well, she needed to be more than a warm, willing body in his bed, a physical release for his sexual desires... a tolerable and practical substitute for some other woman he couldn't have. Every ounce of pride she possessed revolted against that latter prospect. The knowledge was too fresh, too like a drop of acid burning into her flesh for cooler reasoning to play any part in her response. She had to mean more to him. A loveless, careless joining of bodies in the dark was not enough for her.

'I too have my pride,' Rafael asserted, his intonation tellingly abrasive. 'I want nothing from you that you do not give freely. When the pious high of self-denial loses its attractions, you can make the running——'

'Never!' She practically spat the word at him, she was so outraged.

'But you will have no other choice. It will become rather cold and lonely on that side of the bed.'

There was something alarmingly threatening about that blithe promise. It set her teeth on edge. A little while later, she listened to the deep, even sound of his breathing. He had fallen asleep. How could he do that when she was tossing and turning in turmoil? Tears inched a stinging path of betrayal from beneath her lashes. Rafael had offered neither reassurance nor persuasion. If anything, he had sounded bored. He couldn't really have wanted her that much to begin with, and it was not that she wanted him to want her when she most definitely didn't want him, but...? At that point she withdrew from her hopelessly entangled thoughts, experienced a surge of totally illogical fury over his ability to simply drop off to sleep and curled up in a tight ball at the furthest edge of the bed.

'You must be formally introduced to the family,' Doña Isabel repeated immovably.

'But while you're unwell...' Sarah murmured worriedly but her arguments were steadily losing force. It was very obvious that they were unwelcome.

'I have already listened to Rafael on this topic. I am feeling stronger,' Doña Isabel asserted firmly. 'We will hold a dinner party. I have already begun drawing up the guest list. I shall make use of Rafael's secretary, Señora Morales. It will be excellent experience for you as well, Sarah, to see how such things are correctly organised.'

Sarah bent her head, hiding a smile at the thought of the amount of training she had received from her mother. Setting up a dinner party would not have provided her with any problems whatsoever. 'Yes,' she agreed.

'The invitations will go out tomorrow.' Her keen old eyes rested on Sarah. 'You should be with Rafael in the evenings, not sitting here with me.'

Sarah tautened, taken by surprise. 'He's probably in the studio.'

'Consuelo informs me that many nights he sleeps there.'

'He's painting,' Sarah said tightly.

'He is restless, discontented. These are not good signs. Rafael? He needs careful handling. A clever woman would not let him know that he is being handled,' Doña Isabel continued meaningfully.

In the mood Rafael was in at the moment a clever woman would need a shotgun to get that close to him. A bubble of hysterical laughter was trapped in her throat. She had been ill prepared for his grandmother's candour although goodness knew why. Over the past two weeks she had become pretty well acquainted with Doña Isabel. Rafael's grandmother had spent a lifetime dominating her family. While she did not make the mistake of trying to dominate Rafael, she was not above speaking her mind to Sarah in no uncertain terms.

'We've been apart for a long time. There's bound to be—er—teething problems,' Sarah said, opting for a bold retort.

'This is a problem I would place my teeth in quickly.' Doña Isabel had a nice touch with irony. 'I suspect that Rafael is spending his nights with a bottle of tequila.'

'Tequila?' This was news to Sarah.

'He should be spending them with his wife.'

Flags of mortified colour burnished Sarah's cheeks. This was all Rafael's fault and so she intended to tell him. 'You think he's drinking?' she just couldn't help prompting.

Doña Isabel dealt her a haughty look of reproach. 'You misunderstand me. Rafael does not have intemperate habits. But...' her lips pursed anxiously '...there is a wildness in him, a darkness which none of my children had. He must have taken this from his mother. What he feels, he feels too strongly. It disturbs me.'

'It's the artistic temperament,' Sarah soothed.

'I do not believe in artistic temperaments,' Doña Isabel informed her. 'Rafael is merely a little unconventional in his behaviour occasionally. This too he obviously takes from his mother.'

After pressing the bell to bring the nurse at the old lady's request, Sarah wandered aimlessly downstairs. Consuelo was clearing the coffee-cups from the *sala*. Rafael hadn't even touched his, Sarah recalled with growing annoyance. Once the twins were in bed, Rafael disappeared. If they talked at all over dinner, they talked about Gilly and Ben or something strictly impersonal but not about anything that really mattered. If he came to bed at all it was in the early hours and he still rose as usual at sunrise.

In contrast the hours of daylight had been packed with hectic family activity. Rafael had taken them all over the estate. He had also taken them to Cordoba... Granada...Seville. The twins had bounced and skipped exuberantly through the rich pageant of Andalucía's

Moorish heritage. Rafael could bring history alive in a marvellously entertaining way. Sarah had endeavoured to enter fully into the spirit of the occasion and when the children were around Rafael was full of charm and sweetness and light. Gilly and Ben would not suspect for one moment that there was anything wrong between their parents but Sarah knew it every time Rafael looked at her and didn't quite seem to see her, every time he carefully avoided touching her.

In turning away from him that night she had made the biggest mistake she had ever made in her life. Only now was she appreciating that before she had sunk for the space of twenty-four hours into the depths of embittered self-pity and resentment they had been growing close, closer than they had ever been before. Never mind the arguments or the hot exchanges of conflicting opinions. Weren't those the perfect vehicle for saying all those things she had always wanted to say to him but had never had the nerve to say?

And she understood herself, at least, better now. Holding Rafael at an emotional distance had made her feel safer but he moved too far, too fast... he crowded her, sent her imagination off on wild forays into the unknown. From where had she received the idea that he might love another woman? Since when had she become such an acute observer that she read minds? She had no facts on which to base the suspicion and the more she thought about it the more unlikely that suspicion seemed. Rafael was not of the stuff of which martyrs were made.

Yet what had she done? She had let jealousy rise to monstrous proportions in her stupid head. By the time Rafael had slid in positive innocence into that bed, the other woman she had dreamt up had had a face and it had been the face of that woman in New York, that face that was so indelibly imprinted on her memory banks. Someone impossibly glamorous with diamonds in her ears, someone who could emerge with complete cool from a married man's hotel room at dawn without even looking crumpled, someone who was married herself and didn't even seem to care when a photographer caught her full face. Rafael's sort of woman, she had often thought bitterly. Brazen, unashamed.

Blinking rapidly, Sarah was shaken by the effect that that episode could still have on her. And it wasn't healthy to brood and burn with pain over something that happened so long ago. They had both been very young and other couples managed to keep their marriages together despite the disloyalty of one partner, didn't they? Rafael wasn't like her father; he never had been. It wasn't his fault that he couldn't walk a hundred yards without attracting enthralled female attention. So why was she still punishing him? And she was punishing him still, she realised that now.

'Can I get you something, *señora?*' Consuelo gave her a concerned and questioning glance from the door of the *sala*.

'A bottle of tequila,' Sarah said with sudden decision.

'Tequila, *señora?*' Consuelo was aghast and then her homely face reddened fiercely. '*Si, señora, en seguida.*'

Sarah smiled. 'I'm not angry, Consuelo.'

'I worry for him, *señora,*' Consuelo muttered apologetically.

Sarah collected the bottle and went back up to her room. She knew exactly what she was going to put on. The mistake. Karen had nagged her into buying it the previous summer. It had never been worn. She had only packed it out of guilt. It was a scarlet effort with shoestring straps, a low-cut, laced neckline and an above the knee narrow skirt. If it had been in Karen's size, she would have been flattened in the stampede.

Disconcertingly, Rafael was not slumped on the studio sofa with a glass in his hand and the air of anybody feeling anything too strongly. He was painting, and so intent was he in what he was doing that he didn't see her hovering, suddenly feeling grossly underdressed. He had produced a series of internationally acclaimed portrayals of gypsy life and this canvas was clearly another set to join the hall of fame. A clutch of dirty, handsome children were begging with hungry but curiously hard eyes. It was not a comfortable painting. Few of his paintings were.

'Hi,' she said depositing the bottle on the window sill.

'To what...' as he took in the outfit, he faltered '...do I owe the honour?'

Had she really raced out here thinking that he might be miserably drinking himself into oblivion all on his own? Had there been something highly alcoholic in her coffee after dinner? Elegantly clad in beautifully cut khaki cotton trousers and a loose-knit Armani sweater in cream, Rafael looked as extravagantly gorgeous and as alarmingly cool and detached as he had over dinner.

The silence was beginning to stretch to an uneasy length. He was still raking questioning eyes over the scarlet dress. Her knees began to feel exposed, to say nothing of the rest of her. 'Your grandmother's very set on this dinner,' she said hurriedly. 'From what she said, I gathered that you were originally against the idea.'

'For months she has been telling us that she is on her deathbed. Once I agreed with that premise and urged her not to over-exert herself, she suddenly became very keen to prove me wrong.' He set his paintbrush down, still watching her keenly. 'Don't let her suspect that you could arrange the dinner without her assistance.'

'I'm not stupid.'

'I know you are not but she needs to feel necessary. Which of us does not?'

Sarah took a deep breath. 'She's worried about you.'

'Why should she? Ah!' A faint glimmer of contempt coloured his gaze. 'What are you trying to say, Sarah? I believe we can dispense with *Abuela* as a mouthpiece.'

Unfortunately, Sarah was already primed for her next sentence and keen to get it off her chest. 'She thinks you're avoiding me.'

His beautifully expressive eyes, alight with bitter amusement, were veiled by dense black lashes. 'So, I have *Abuela* to thank for your unexpected visit.'

'No. You don't,' she protested. 'It was an impulse. Maybe boredom with my own company drove me out here in desperation.'

An ebony brow quirked. 'Did it?'

Sarah was not feeling as forgiving as she had felt ten minutes earlier. Rafael was not helping her out. Olive branches were supposed to be graciously received and he was standing there emanating positive waves of ungracious antagonism. 'It's a possibility, isn't it?' she snapped defensively.

'Why did you change out of the outfit you were wearing at dinner?'

Two could play at this game, she decided. 'I spilt coffee on it.'

'Why did you bring a bottle of tequila?'

'Maybe I felt like a drink!' Sarah was steadily becoming more and more annoyed.

'Do you like tequila?'

'Why shouldn't I?' Sarah tilted her chin challengingly. 'Where do you keep your glasses?'

'In the kitchen.' Crossing the floor, he swiped the tequila off the sill and strode gracefully out into the hall.

'Do you want it straight?' he enquired smoothly.

'Why not?' she called on the 'in for a penny, in for a pound' principle.

He thrust a glass in her hand, knocked his own against it in salutation. 'Let us drink to straight speech.'

It struck Sarah as a very odd version of 'cheers' but she plastered on a smile and took a gallant gulp. 'Not bad,' she said chirpily. 'Straight speech? When I first came here, I told myself it was only for the twins——'

'Do I hold you prisoner? Do you see chains? Bars?' He let fly at her without giving her the slightest warning of his intent.

'You have a very nasty temper.' Not surprisingly, Sarah had retreated several feet.

'*Dios,* do you wonder at it?' he grated.

Sarah breathed in slowly and carefully. 'You expected too much of me too soon. That's what you always do, Rafael. When you want something, you want it yesterday. I don't like being railroaded into major decisions. I needed time. And time is something you have never given me!'

'I have left you alone, Sarah. What more do you want?'

She bent her head. In the mood he was in, she couldn't quite pluck up the courage to tell him that that wasn't what she wanted at all. 'I've had one shock after another since I arrived. You kept too many secrets from me and I can't say that that makes me feel secure.'

'You forget that I kept those secrets from you seven years ago. If I had not, you would have tried to change me,' he condemned harshly. 'In my life, I have endured too many such attempts. Did you appreciate then how much I needed to paint? Had you known of my background, would you not have tried to persuade me to heal the breach with Felipe and spend the rest of my days pushing paperwork in an office? Or would you have accepted me as I was?'

She could not argue the points he had made. Parental approval had meant a great deal to her then. Without realising what she might be doing to Rafael, she probably would have been keen for him to mend fences with his grandfather and put on a three-piece suit and join the business world, reasoning that he could still continue to paint in his spare time if he wanted to. She sighed, too honest to deny the truth. 'You're right. You always have an answer, don't you?'

'If I had, we wouldn't have broken up.'

The dialogue was straying into dangerous waters she had not planned to touch. She was very pale. 'We broke up,' she said shakily, 'because you went to bed with another woman.'

'You are very sure of that,' he breathed fiercely.

'One hundred per cent sure,' Sarah returned, her fingernails cutting painfully into the palm of her clenched hand. 'You wanted to hurt me and you did. Let's leave it at that.'

'I have never wanted to hurt you in my life and I have never lied to you either.'

Sarah shook her head vehemently. 'And that's exactly why you've never mentioned it, because you can't lie about it and I don't want any explanation. It would make me hate you,' she confided truthfully. 'In fact if you so much as mention that woman I'll walk out of this room right now.'

He was white with anger. 'You judged me unseen, unheard!'

'And you did exactly the same thing to me with a lot less justification,' she reminded him sadly. 'There's no point in talking about all that now.'

'At least I didn't run away. You may not have been well but you were carrying my child. You owed me more than your parents' lies. You wouldn't even let me see you!'

Abruptly, Sarah sank down on the sofa with its multi-coloured pile of cushions. The taunt about running away had stung hard. 'I didn't have a choice.'

'You could have phoned me from your sickbed, sent a postcard! Anything! But you did nothing and you knew I didn't know where you were.'

'But I did expect you to make it your business to find out when I vanished off the face of the earth.' Sarah held her head high. 'I think it's time that I told you the whole story. The day I found out about your affair, all hell broke loose. I didn't handle the news the way my father hoped I would. I was hysterical and in the midst of a very unpleasant scene I fell on the stairs. I was badly bruised and I started to bleed,' she enumerated flatly. 'I thought I was losing the baby and that didn't make me any calmer. The doctor sedated me. When I was told I had to have bed rest, I accepted it. I thought I would have to go into hospital but it was a private clinic. What I didn't know was that my father had told our elderly GP that I had thrown myself down the stairs.'

Rafael's anger had evaporated. He was listening intently, his dark features taut and strained. 'Why should he tell such a lie?'

Sarah didn't answer him. Her slender body was rigid with tension. 'My father owned a large stake in Twelvetrees. The doctor in charge was a personal friend. I was actually in there a few days before I realised that it wasn't just a nursing home. The lady in the room next door was as nutty as fruitcake. That's why she was there. She was quite harmless but she was probably quite an embarrassment to her wealthy relatives. I was in there because I had supposedly attempted to kill myself and my unborn child and my poor distracted father did not know what else he could do with me.'

'Infierno!' Rafael was ashen pale, incredulous comprehension starting to glimmer in his appalled gaze. 'But why, why should he have done this to you? It makes no sense!'

'It makes perfect sense,' Sarah contradicted. 'It got me out of the way. He was determined to keep us apart. He actually tried to make me believe that I was sick and that he was only doing what was best for me. He wanted me to divorce you and I wouldn't sign the papers. In the end I signed because it just didn't matter any more.'

Rafael closed his anguished eyes for a split second. 'How long? For how long were you there?'

'Nine weeks. I wasn't badly treated. I don't want you to think that. I had a beautiful room, regular meals and free therapy thrown in.' Her voice cracked slightly. 'For nine weeks, nothing I said was believed by the staff. They humoured me, thought I couldn't face up to what I'd tried to do! My father wanted you out of my life and there was nothing he wouldn't have done to win. It had become a personal vendetta between him and you. I was just the unlucky bystander who had to pick up the tab. No, forget I said that. It isn't fair because you didn't know,' she completed huskily. 'You never got my letter.'

'Letter?' Rafael queried jerkily, still visibly appalled by the realisation that he could have prevented her father from putting her into the clinic.

'It was never posted. My father saw to that.' Her tense mouth tightened.

'What was in it this letter?' he probed.

'I wanted to see you ... to talk.'

Rafael stifled a curse. 'Your father has much to answer to me for. When we are next in England, we will face your parents together.'

Sarah shook her head uncertainly. 'I really don't know why I told you about all this.'

He expelled his breath raggedly. 'You should have told me at the beginning.'

She produced a shadowy smile. 'You said you would take Gilly and Ben away from me,' she reminded him. 'I spent nine weeks in that place. How do you think that would have looked in court?'

Rafael flinched, a nerve tugging at the edge of his compressed mouth. 'You thought of that?'

'I thought of nothing else,' she whispered. 'I don't think I had a single night of uninterrupted sleep until I came here. It was only then that I really believed that you weren't going to try to put me out of their lives.'

There was a faint tremor in his hand as he lifted his glass and drained it. He was still very pale, almost drawn, his cheekbones blunt angles protruding beneath his skin. 'Sarah, you must believe that I had no idea you had this pressure on you. I never wanted to take you to court and I never seriously considered for longer than one insane hour doing anything so cruel as to separate you from Ben and Gilly.'

A watery smile formed on her tense mouth. 'You didn't give that impression.'

'I was very bitter, Sarah.' He parted eloquent hands as if he could not otherwise emphasise just how bitter he had been. 'How can you understand what believing that you had killed our child did to me? It made me hate you. But it also made me hate myself. I felt responsible for what I believed you had done. How could I not feel responsible? For me it was like a punishment for loving you too much, for making you unhappy in spite of that love.' His expressive mouth clenched hard. 'I cannot bear to think of you locked in this place you describe.'

'It wasn't that bad. Monotonous, but since I had to rest anyway——'

'Don't make a joke of it. You must have been terrified! Then, you were not the woman you are now.' He thrust brown fingers roughly through his already tousled black hair, wreaking further havoc and provoking a torturous pang of tenderness inside her. 'You were so fragile you used to scare me but when we parted I would not let myself remember that. In my mind, I made you into a heartless bitch I could hate! I blamed you for everything.'

'That's normal,' she said, taking another appreciative sip of her drink. 'I like this.'

Unexpectedly, he smiled at her, one of those gloriously spine-tinglingly sensual smiles. 'That is not tequila that you are drinking. Tequila would put you flat on your back.'

That was the closest thing to a promising suggestion he had made in two weeks. She looked at him hopefully but it was very obvious as the smile slid away that he was not thinking along the same lines.

'Do you know why I came here tonight?'

'*Abuela* embarrassed you into coming. It's all right,' he dismissed wryly. 'I am not angry about it.'

He was anything but pleased about it though and she hid a smile. 'I intended to tell you that I was . . . well, that I was agreeable to...' Already she was losing the thread, suddenly plunged into tongue-tied inadequacy at the fear that he very possibly might not want the assurances she planned to give.

'Agreeable to what?'

'To having a normal marriage...to trying again. I only needed some time to think the idea over.' It wasn't quite coming out with the flavour she had intended.

'So you thought it over. That was very sensible of you,' he conceded flatly, unappreciative of the news. 'But then that is you. It is not me. You would not want to be guilty of haste or enthusiasm but then it is obvious that you do not feel this is necessary. What did I pass on?'

Sarah was studying him bemusedly. 'I beg your pardon?'

'While you were for two weeks weighing up whether or not you would stay? Surely I entered these pros and cons somewhere?' Golden eyes were pinned to her with restrained fury. 'Two weeks, it takes you. It didn't take me twenty-four hours to make the same decision!'

Sarah swallowed hard, unable to understand why on earth he should be angry. 'But as you pointed out a minute ago, I am not you. If you must know, it never occurred to me that I had the choice of not staying unless I planned to return to England without Gilly and Ben.'

He stared at her, a blaze of emotion in his brilliant eyes. 'Leave them out of this!'

Sarah belatedly grasped what had infuriated him and she wasn't surrendering, no way was she! He didn't like the idea that she might be staying solely for the twins' benefit. On the other hand, he hadn't balked at dragging her all the way to Spain and keeping her yoked to the same humiliating belief. 'You weighed heavily in the pros and cons.'

'I do not want to be weighed like a sack of grain,' he flashed back at her rawly. 'I do not weigh you.'

Sarah could see a roaring attack of artistic temperament threatening on the horizon and as she absorbed the driven tension tautening his lean, powerful length, she registered, finally understood on a surge of disbelief that what she felt for him was of such overwhelming importance that he was painfully and unmistakably bracing himself for words that would hurt, words that would wound. Her heart turned over inside her breast and did a double back-flip for good measure. Suddenly she felt incredibly generous.

'Why do you think I'm wearing this stupid dress? I came here to—er—seduce you,' she confided tensely.

'*Qué?*' he muttered, shaken by the announcement.

'I thought a drink might help. I hadn't quite thought out ways and means and when it comes down to it I'm really not that sure what I'm supposed to do,' she admitted curtly, a stricken look in her eyes.

Rafael was breathing shallowly, rather like someone who had raced up a hill expecting to find a spectacularly rewarding view only to find it blocked at the very last minute. 'You want to go to bed with me,' he translated fiercely. 'As if I was just anybody?'

Sarah was stunned, momentarily quite bemused by this disconcerting response. But as the full force of his derision hit her, it was absolutely the last straw. Anger and pain roared through her in a blaze as she leapt upright. 'Right now, just anybody sounds a lot more tempting!' she told him furiously. 'How can you be so blind? I wouldn't dream of going to bed with you if I didn't love you! I wouldn't do it to keep you and I wouldn't do it even to keep the children. It takes more than a couple of glasses of wine to make me forget my principles. It takes you, and if you think I'm pleased about that, you're crazy!'

CHAPTER TEN

'THAT'S a hell of a way to tell me that you love me,' Rafael breathed hoarsely.

Maddeningly aware that instead of slapping him down hard she had inexplicably strayed into doing exactly the opposite by betraying herself, Sarah was, if anything, even more furious than she had been a moment earlier. 'You had your chance and you blew it!' she told him wrathfully. 'And don't you ever dare to refer to this again. As far as I'm concerned, tonight never happened!'

'But why should we want to forget it?' A brilliant smile had transformed his dark features. 'After all, I am also in love with you.'

'I suppose it just sneaked up on you a second ago!'

'*Por dios, querida*—I love you!' he declared fiercely.

'I suppose that's why you've been sleeping down here, treating me like a piece of furniture or something...' Her throat was closing over, clogged with tears and bitterness and a whole host of other emotions, a desperate desire to believe in him, rigorously thrust by fear to the very bottom of the pile.

'Or someone whom I cannot be near ever without wanting to touch,' he completed softly. 'You said you didn't want me.'

'I thought you were in love with someone else.'

'Who is this someone else?'

'How should I know?' It was an embarrassed wail. 'When I asked you what would happen if you did fall in love, you looked sort of... well, you looked like you were hiding something.'

'Of course I was hiding something! How do you think it felt for you to ask such a question as if it didn't matter a damn to you?' he demanded. 'It hurt because I loved you. Sarah,' he said her name achingly as though he savoured every syllable individually and her lower limbs went weak but she fought off the sensation in panic.

'I want to believe you, but——'

'No but.' A forefinger rested reprovingly against her tremulous lips. 'I am willing to spend the rest of my life proving it beyond a doubt. In England, I told you that the very first night I knew what I would do. I knew I still loved you and I didn't want to admit it.' He was winding a set of very determined arms round her and wonderful floaty feelings were interfering drastically with her concentration. 'But all I could think about was this man with his hands on you.'

'What about that creature pawing you at the party?' Sarah gasped, not so easily silenced.

'I am not in the habit of being pawed in public.' A dark flush had settled on his cheekbones. 'Now, it sounds very childish but I was not sorry that you should see that another woman should find me attractive. It was pride, it was——'

'Disgusting,' Sarah supplied pitilessly but she was reassured.

Disorientatingly, he grinned down at her. 'Your feelings showed and I couldn't understand why it should bother you. It made me think, it made me follow you home——'

'You followed Gordon's car?'

'I didn't think about what I was doing and your reactions to me were very confusing,' he murmured tautly. 'And then Gilly came in and after that, for me it is just a blank that evening. I don't even remember what I said. I was devastated.'

Sarah was discovering that the Armani sweater was worn next to bare skin. Her hands had crept beneath the welt to smooth covetously over warm, hair-roughened flesh. Satisfyingly, he shuddered against her. His fingers suddenly meshed into her silky hair, jerking her head back so that his mouth could possess hers with a voracious hunger and unleashed restraint that threatened to knock her off her feet. Breathing hard, he released her bruised lips and muttered something fiercely apologetic in Spanish.

'Twice, we have made love,' he groaned. 'And twice, I have lost control and behaved like an uncivilised brute. This time, it won't be like that.'

'You lost control? I thought you were experimenting.'

He swept her up in his arms with a grin. 'I thought you were experimenting with me. I nearly took you in the hall, I was so incredibly excited.' He frowned, tensed. 'This is crude?'

'Wonderful,' she whispered in urgent contradiction against his cheek. 'Say it again. You can be as uncivilised as you like.'

He deposited her on a single bed in a bare, almost monastic little room. He smoothed her rucked skirt very carefully down over her slim thighs. 'This cocktail I mixed has gone straight to your head. I do not think I should share this bed with you tonight.'

'Why not?' Snatched cruelly from her haze of wonderfully wanton anticipation, she clutched a handful of his sweater to keep him beside her.

'Tomorrow, you may feel I took advantage of you. I can wait.' Wildly impatient and hungry dark eyes slammed into hers and hurriedly veiled. 'I can give you time. This is not as important as you think to me. You must be very sure that this is what you want.'

'I want you.' Dampness stinging her eyelids, she blinked fiercely. 'I want you so much.'

'*Enamorada . . . te quiero, te quiero,*' he intoned raggedly, accepting her invitation with an exciting lack of restraint.

He had taught her of pleasure that teased and pleasure that burned and this time he taught her of pleasure that had no limits, pleasure that went on and on and on until she cried out his name, caught up and controlled by the storm of passion and flung gloriously over the edge of the horizon.

He was covering her hot face with kisses when she recovered, talking in a riveting mix of Spanish and English, and there was a lot about how much he loved her, how he couldn't bear to live without her, how he would never let her out of his sight again. It was heaven, absolute heaven. She lay there drinking it all in, dazed, exhilarated, punch drunk on the amazing knowledge that he was hers, absolutely, irrevocably hers, retrieved at the eleventh hour from the very jaws of death...or whatever you called all those ravenous other women out there, she reflected, feeling a lot more charitable towards those faceless hordes. No competition now.

'In the morning, we can fly to Madrid,' he murmured between slightly less teasing kisses, a communicable tension in his hard, muscular length.

'Madrid?'

'We have a townhouse there.' He met her still-dreaming eyes with just the smallest hint of apprehension. 'Caterina lives and works in Madrid. I would like you to meet her.'

'Can't it wait a day or two?'

'Caterina is not the type to intrude.' He was practically telepathic in interpreting her lukewarm response and she felt instantly mean and over-possessive. 'The children can stay here and join us later in the week if they miss us.'

'If?' she queried.

'Our children are very self-sufficient.'

There was no arguing with fact. 'What age is your cousin?' she asked curiously.

'Two years my senior.'

'She's divorced, isn't she?'

He sighed. 'About eight years ago, she let Lucía browbeat her into marrying a very rich American. She is not like her mother and Lucía has always given her a hard time. Gerry wasn't much better for her ego. He beat her up regularly.'

'Oh, lord,' Sarah breathed in horror.

'Early in their marriage, his violence cost her the child she was carrying. She had a nervous breakdown,' Rafael volunteered. 'She recovered but Lucía didn't want her to get a divorce. Not only was there the question of religion but also the loss of Gerry's money. Caterina had signed a pre-nuptial contract. In the event of a divorce, she got virtually nothing. When she confided in me, I persuaded her to leave Gerry. I gave her the strength to do it.'

'I'm glad. Thank goodness she did listen to you.' Sarah was warmly sympathetic. 'Lucía really is a horror, isn't she?'

They flew to Madrid on a company jet. Sarah was feeling happy, so happy that she was almost afraid. She had that 'on a roller-coaster' sensation and it was a very long time since she had last let her emotions control her to that extent.

'I ought to tell you about my years in Truro.' A rueful smile curved her mouth. 'We shouldn't have any secrets from each other.'

It seemed to her that Rafael became marginally less at ease within seconds. In fact, come to think of it—and she didn't really want to think of it—he might be lounging in a relaxed fashion but ever since they had climbed aboard the jet there had been an odd indefinable tension in the atmosphere, a tension that for some reason best known to himself he was working hard to conceal.

'But you have nothing to explain to me,' he sighed. 'I was very much in the wrong and I had no right to speak to you as I did. It was wondrously generous of you to tell me the truth.'

She looked at him in surprise. 'You did believe me?'

'You have always told me the truth but I am very stubborn when an idea becomes fixed in my head,' he acknowledged, tawny eyes resting on her with faint amusement. 'I am also very jealous and I had never had to be jealous of you before. It did me no harm. Now you can tell me about Truro.'

He was very quiet and low-key. Her brow furrowed. What was wrong with him? And then she felt awful, really awful for forgetting how he felt about flying. Bless him, she thought guiltily, he still hadn't got over that phobia and he was predictably set on being macho for her benefit. Admitting to fear was Rafael's biggest problem. Admitting to irrational fear was quite impossible for him. On the first flight she had ever shared with him he had pretended to sleep and she had been fooled until he staggered on to solid ground again, grey-faced and drained. Since then he had improved enormously and she would have liked to tell him that, but felt that tact required her to draw no attention to what he was experiencing.

Instead she began to talk, hoping to take his mind off things. Inconsequential chatter, however, did not provide much of a diversion. His responses were monosyllabic and, in the end, she fell silent. A limousine collected them at the airport. Sarah stole a glance at the tension that was now squarely etched in his features and took a deep breath. 'You probably don't want me to mention this but I think it would be easier if you just talked about it.'

A line formed between his ebony brows. 'Talked about what?'

'Your phobia about flying,' she said gently.

'My what?' He looked at her in astonishment and then suddenly grinned disarmingly. 'Sarah, I got over that years ago.'

She had to glue her tongue to the roof of her mouth. If that was how he wanted to play it, she guessed that she was expected to abide by the rules. The townhouse was not what she had naïvely expected. It was a mansion set behind imposingly high walls, not the convenient little *pied-à-terre* of her imagining.

A manservant opened double doors that gave on to an impressive marble tiled hall. Marble busts on pedestals and Ionic columns vied for her attention.

'It's like a museum,' Rafael breathed unappreciatively. 'My grandparents used this house as their permanent home when I was a child. *Abuela* still prefers it to Alcazar. Felipe also let Caterina stay here until she found an apartment.' He paused. 'I've invited her to join us here for lunch.'

'Fine.' But Sarah's mind had taken a very feminine jump on to what one might wear to meet a fashion designer. 'I think I'll freshen up.'

'I have some calls to make.'

A maid showed her up to their bedroom. Sarah absorbed the massive baroque splendour of the gilded and heavily draped four-poster bed with wide eyes. It was something of a surprise to find a completely up to date bathroom next door. Laying out an elegant Yves St Laurent suit, she began to undress. She was grateful that she had taken the time in Seville to add a few extras to her wardrobe. The fitted V-necked top and flowing skirt in soft complementary shades of grey, purple and blue were very flattering against her light hair and the tan she had acquired.

As she reached the head of the stairs, she heard the front doors opening and Rafael strode out into the hall. A woman hurried to greet him. He stretched out his hands and she gripped them, leaning forward to kiss him Continental fashion on both cheeks. It was only as she drew back that Sarah drew in her breath sharply.

Her fingers tightened bone-white on the banister. Shock was rippling through her in waves. Her heart was thumping like a trip hammer. It couldn't be the same woman, it simply couldn't be. How good could her recall be of a photograph she had only seen once five years ago? This woman looked smaller, thinner. Her tumbled dark curls were shorter, held back by ivory combs. They were still holding hands, talking in low urgent voices, entirely intent on each other.

Very slowly, Sarah released her grip on the banister and retreated several steps back on to the landing. She was terrified of being seen. Caterina. Rafael's cousin. Once married to an American. His silence now made a horrible kind of sense and of course he didn't necessarily know that there had been a photograph, did he? Caterina had been the woman with him in that hotel room, the woman who had destroyed her marriage, the woman who had caused her untold pain and suffering. It was definitely her and most ironically she was not as beautiful as Sarah had made her in her memory. Her features were too strong for beauty but she was very attractive.

She made it back to the bedroom without realising that she had gone there. Gazing blankly round the room, she made an effort to pull herself together. It didn't work. What the heck was going on? What had she got herself into? Rafael expected her to sit down to lunch with this woman. To say that at the very least that was tacky of him was to be generous. Incredibly generous. Her stomach heaved.

'Aren't you ready yet?' Rafael was in the doorway, sleek and elegant in a lightweight dark grey suit. 'Caterina has arrived early.'

'I saw her.' Bitter anger shuddered through her and, with it, a sickening sense of betrayal. 'And I recognised her.'

'So there was a photograph,' he said thoughtfully. 'Papa was most thorough. I should have been prepared for that possibility.'

Wide-eyed with disbelief, Sarah stared at him. 'You weren't prepared? May you rot in hell for this!' she launched in disgust.

His tawny eyes flared, his strong jawline clenching. He thrust the door closed. 'I have the feeling that you are going to disappoint me. Caterina can entertain herself for a few minutes.'

'You think *I* am going to disappoint *you?*' Her voice was shaking and she couldn't stop it shaking. 'You are so right, Rafael! If there hadn't been a photograph, I wouldn't have known...'

Being found out did not appear to bother him in the slightest. His narrow-eyed scrutiny was cool. 'But what do you know, Sarah?'

She bent her head in an agony of pain, quivering with the force of her emotions. 'I know that I will never trust you again. How could you bring her here?' she gasped. 'Is there some continuing affair that makes it worthwhile? Or does it give you some sort of a thrill to sit down to lunch with your mistress and your wife?'

'No, it does not give me a thrill, because Caterina has never been my mistress,' he imparted shortly. 'I would still like to know why an hour or two alone in a hotel room constitutes indisputable evidence of infidelity.'

'It's sufficient for a divorce!' Sarah flung wildly. 'If you're still trying to insist that there's some other explanation, I'm afraid that I'm not even going to listen to it.'

'You're going to listen all right,' Rafael grated rawly. 'You don't trust me. You do not even make the slightest attempt to even pretend that you trust me. But how very gracious of you to forgive and forget something which I didn't do!'

'I can't believe that!' There was a slight sob in the assurance. 'I'll never believe that.'

'Tell me, Sarah, what sort of man would introduce his mistress to his wife?' he demanded fiercely. 'Is that how you see me? I wanted you to know the truth in the kindest possible way without distressing Caterina. I didn't know there was a photograph. I wanted you to meet. I intended to lead the conversation in a certain direction and leave you to do your own detective work. And how were you to achieve that? By asking me. Not by behaving like the hysterical insecure adolescent you were five years ago when it happened!'

Blind fury was beginning to take hold of Sarah. 'If you don't get out of here, I am going to lose my head!' she warned.

He slashed an enraged hand through the air. 'Caterina came to the gallery to see me. It was three years since I had seen her. I didn't know how her marriage turned out. We had a lot to catch up on and I took her back to my hotel. I took her to my room because she was crying, Sarah. No doubt you would have expected me to make her sit in the public bar in that state!' he condemned. 'She told me about Gerry and we sat up talking into the early hours of the morning. He was away on business at the time and she was all wound up because he was due back later that day. Are you listening to me, Sarah?'

His voice cracked across the room like a whiplash and her head jerked up, complete confusion in her eyes. 'You could tell me anything,' she whispered, refusing to let the conviction of years be torn away and destroyed within seconds.

'I am telling you everything,' he gritted roughly. 'When I heard what he had been doing to her, I told her to get out because he wasn't going to stop. She had confided in no one but Lucía. She desperately needed someone to tell her that it was not the most wicked thing in the world for her to leave him. And I did it. She decided to sell her jewellery and fly home to Spain where she eventually sought refuge with my grandparents.'

Tiny little tremors of shock were quivering through her. His raw explanation was sinking in word by word like stones settling to the bottom of a turbulent pond. 'Is this true?' she muttered, scarcely knowing what she was saying.

'*Dios,* do you still think I am telling lies? What do I have to do to establish my innocence?' Golden eyes fierce as a hawk's slammed into her. 'Caterina has no idea of what that night cost me. It cost me my marriage. It cost me my children. And I wouldn't hurt her with that knowledge. Let me be the one to remove any lingering doubts that you might have.'

Sarah sank down heavily on a chair because her legs felt hollow. 'You don't need to say any more. I believe you.'

He expelled his breath in a pent-up rush and sighed. '*Lucía* was pregnant when my father jilted her. That is why Ramón married her...'

Sarah looked up dazedly. 'But that means——'

'She's my half-sister.'

Sarah swallowed hard as the final pieces fell into place. It explained the depth of Lucía's bitterness, her harshness towards her only daughter.

'But not according to her birth certificate,' Rafael continued drily. 'Publicly she was a premature baby. I think it's time we rejoined our guest.'

Sarah's head jerked up in dismay. 'I can't face her like this!'

Rafael closed a powerful hand over hers, forcing her upright. 'Think of it as penance.'

'You can't blame me for what I thought,' she gasped strickenly. 'Why are you so angry? I thought what anybody would have thought.'

'You are not anybody,' he countered thinly. 'You are my wife. I wanted you to ask me what had happened that night. I wanted you to ask yourself now whether I would have done such a thing to you.'

If he was trying to make her feel horribly guilty, he was succeeding. 'I'm sorry.'

'No doubt I am unfashionably idealistic but I want you to get one fact straight in your head for all time,' he snapped. 'I am not promiscuous. I am not a womaniser. I like women but I don't flirt with them. When I'm with you, I don't even look at other women.'

He trailed her down the stairs and swept her in to meet Caterina without pause.

'I have been so excited about meeting you,' Caterina confided warmly as she rose from her seat. 'It's a long time ago but Rafael once told me so much about you and he made me very curious.' She exchanged a rueful glance with Rafael. 'Do you remember that night? I was full of my troubles and you were trying to cheer me up by telling me about Sarah.'

Lunch was over and Caterina was gone before the hectic flush had completely died from her complexion. The last fear and the last cloud had vanished from her horizon but it had left a nasty after-taste in her mouth. At last she understood something of the emotions that had seethed in Rafael when he had met her again and she marvelled that he could still say that he loved her. Or was he still saying it? He had wanted her to doubt his guilt for herself. And she had let him down, there was no denying that. Now that she knew the truth, she wondered why she had ever doubted him.

He had never lied to her, never, ever lied to her—but he had been much too proud to actually deny his infidelity. All he had done was hint about extenuating circumstances and that had merely fitted in with what she had assumed had happened. And after five years of ingrained bitter acceptance of his betrayal doubts did not come easily. Why couldn't he just have told her?

Oh, that would have been far too simple for Rafael. He had tried to manipulate her into giving him the response he wanted and if it hadn't been for the photograph he probably would have succeeded.

'Are you going to forgive me?'

She had been studying the bedroom carpet, having whisked herself upstairs as soon as Caterina departed. Her head jerked up, stark pain in her eyes. 'Are *you* going to forgive *me?*'

'Sarah, if you killed me, I would forgive you from heaven.' He studied her for a torturous split second and then, with a groan, he bent down and reached for her, hauling her into his arms. 'I've been waiting for you to come downstairs,' he confessed.

'And I've been waiting for you to come up.' With a shaky little laugh she met the tawny eyes sweeping adoringly over her face. 'I trust you, I really do trust you. Do I pass?'

'With honours.' He brought her up against the hungry thrust of his body. 'I just wanted to wipe the slate clean and I got a little carried away with the plot,' he muttered feverishly.

'A little?'

'And a little angry when it didn't work out.' He ravished her parted lips, passed an arm beneath her hips and lifted her all in the same motion. By the time she opened her eyes again she was on the bed. Rafael was surveying it with satisfaction. 'This is a bed for making babies in.'

'P-pardon?'

Dark colour accentuated his hard cheekbones. 'I was thinking out loud.'

Sarah reached up and twisted her arms round his neck. 'Tell me more.'

'You mean——'

'Why not?' She toyed with a black luxuriant strand of hair. 'I'll swamp you with domesticity.'

'Swamp?' he queried.

'Drown.' There was so much tenderness in his eyes that she ached.

'I like to drown with you...to see you fat——'

'What?' she mock shrieked.

'Round,' he adjusted hurriedly but his wide, passionate mouth was sliding into a wicked grin. 'Voluptuous, sexy...' His voice sank to a husky murmur as he moved against her, letting her feel his need, making her quiver deliciously beneath him.

'I love you,' she whispered. 'Are we going to talk all afternoon?'

'I am going to love you all afternoon, *querida*,' he promised huskily. 'All afternoon and forever.'

And he did.

While away the lazy days of late Summer with our new gift selection
Intimate Moments

Four Romances, new in paperback, from four favourite authors.
The perfect treat!

The Colour of the Sea
Rosemary Hammond

Had We Never Loved
Jeneth Murrey

The Heron Quest
Charlotte Lamb

Magic of the Baobab
Yvonne Whittal

Available from July 1991. Price: £6.40

Mills & Boon

Next month's Romances

Each month, you can choose from a world of variety in romance with Mills & Boon. These are the new titles to look out for next month.

DANGEROUS INTERLOPER Penny Jordan

BETRAYED Anne Mather

TEMPT ME NOT Susan Napier

FORBIDDEN ENCHANTMENT Patricia Wilson

STAY UNTIL DAWN Elizabeth Oldfield

LASTING LEGACY Kay Thorpe

FORBIDDEN PASSION Sarah Holland

OUTBACK MAN Miranda Lee

MAN OF TRUTH Jessica Marchant

CARIBBEAN DESIRE Cathy Williams

SHADOW IN THE WINGS Lee Stafford

RISK OF THE HEART Grace Green

THE PARIS TYPE Christine Greig

HEARTSONG Melinda Cross

THE OTHER WOMAN Jessica Steele

STARSIGN
FORTUNE IN THE STARS Kate Proctor

Available from Boots, Martins, John Menzies, W.H. Smith, Woolworths and other paperback stockists.

Also available from Mills and Boon Reader Service, P.O. Box 236, Thornton Road, Croydon, Surrey CR9 3RU.